Lily couldn't se[...] [...] other than kissi[...]

They both seemed to be resisting the pull that had drawn them so close that their lips were almost touching. Then, as if the last thread of restraint had snapped, his lips were suddenly on hers, taking and giving all at once.

Lily was swept up in his arms, the strength of his embrace matched by the ferocity of his kisses. Finn was creating a need inside her she hadn't felt for a long time, an ache only he could fill, but also an awakening of something she knew to be dangerous. To give in to this lust, this want to be with him completely, was not something that could be satisfied by a onetime surrender to temptation.

She couldn't fall for Finn. He had daughters to think about, girls who had already suffered so much loss and grief, to even consider getting involved with someone who couldn't be there for them in the future. It wouldn't be fair on any of them after all this time of denying herself a family to now insinuate herself into someone else's.

Dear Reader,

Everyone loves firefighters, right? Not only are they lifesavers prepared to run into burning buildings at the drop of a hat, but they look pretty good in uniform, too. Hopefully, Finn and Lily's story goes into a deeper side of the occupation and how it affects the families of those men and women who often put their own lives on the line for others.

The idea of sending members of the fire service out on emergency cardiac calls is something that is being trialed in my part of the world and that proves yet again how much our key workers are prepared to do in the hope of saving more lives.

Okay, so my hero, Finn, is reluctant at first to take part in the task…and with good reason. He's concerned the extra responsibility will prove too stressful for his team. It takes a feisty cardiologist and some mediation, not to mention an emergency medical situation, to show him the immediate benefits of getting someone to the scene quickly.

My heroine, Lily, is a fortysomething cakeaholic with a penchant for beachcombing. She's not autobiographical in the slightest…

I hope you enjoy my fiery couple!

Karin xx

SINGLE DAD FOR THE HEART DOCTOR

KARIN BAINE

HARLEQUIN
MEDICAL
ROMANCE

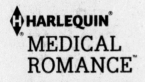

HARLEQUIN®
MEDICAL
ROMANCE™

Recycling programs
for this product may
not exist in your area.

ISBN-13: 978-1-335-73766-3

Single Dad for the Heart Doctor

Copyright © 2023 by Karin Baine

For questions and comments about the quality of this book, please contact us at CustomerService@Harlequin.com.

Harlequin Enterprises ULC
22 Adelaide St. West, 41st Floor
Toronto, Ontario M5H 4E3, Canada
www.Harlequin.com

Printed in U.S.A.

Karin Baine lives in Northern Ireland with her husband, two sons and her out-of-control notebook collection. Her mother and her grandmother's vast collection of books inspired her love of reading and her dream of becoming a Harlequin author. Now she can tell people she has a *proper* job! You can follow Karin on Twitter, @karinbaine1, or visit her website for the latest news—karinbaine.com.

Books by Karin Baine

Harlequin Medical Romance

Carey Cove Midwives

Festive Fling to Forever

Pups that Make Miracles

Their One-Night Christmas Gift

Their One-Night Twin Surprise
Healed by Their Unexpected Family
Reunion with His Surgeon Princess
One Night with Her Italian Doc
The Surgeon and the Princess
The Nurse's Christmas Hero
Wed for Their One Night Baby
A GP to Steal His Heart

Visit the Author Profile page
at Harlequin.com for more titles.

For my lovely neighbors, Stella, Sammy and Miriam.
I'm going to miss you very much. xx

CHAPTER ONE

DEATH NEVER GOT EASIER.

Lily picked up a handful of shingle from the beach, pocketing the frosted, sea-tumbled aquamarine glass and the pottery shards. There were several fragments of blue and white willow-pattern treasures for her to re-purpose along with the glass. The Victorians' rubbish and broken crockery, tossed into the sea, was now her treasure. When she had some free time she'd make it into some jewellery…something beautiful. Give it new life.

She pulled her cardigan tighter around her body as the wind began to pick up, but she didn't mind the cold. This was her happy place, where she could forget her worries and concentrate on spotting little gems and giving new life to those broken pieces. It wasn't so easy in the real world.

Losing a patient was always difficult. In her job as a cardiologist, death was not something she could always conquer and she did her best. But events such as tonight's made her job harder than ever, and reminded her of her own mortality. She had chosen this career path to give people a second chance at life but sometimes, through no fault of her own, she didn't even get to play her part.

The ambulance had taken too long to get to their remote village, Glen Nesbitt, on Northern Ireland's Antrim coast. There hadn't been anywhere close by for the emergency medical helicopter to land, even if it had reached the place in time.

In cardiac cases every second counted and, from her point of view, a thirty-eight-year-old mother of two had died unnecessarily. On this occasion the medical profession had failed her and her family with their poor response time. Lily knew she could have saved the woman if she'd got to her sooner and that would keep her awake tonight.

Usually it was thoughts of her father and her sister—of how she hadn't been able to save them. Of her mother, who had died of a broken heart years later, even without inheriting the condition which had stolen half of their little family. Not least the ticking time bomb in Lily's chest which would eventually take her too.

She had inherited the same faulty gene and now, with her confirmed diagnosis of dilated cardiomyopathy, premature death was something she had to consider. DCM left the heart muscle stretched thin, too weak to contract enough to pump blood properly around the rest of the body.

Her sister hadn't had any warning, suddenly collapsing after they'd been racing along the beach, dying from heart failure before anyone had known there was anything wrong. Lily had been the younger of the two but losing Iris at the age of ten years, then her father only days later, killed by the shock, meant she'd grown up from the age of seven as an only child. Then an orphan from the age of seventeen when her mother passed away too.

They'd been unaware of the deadly spectre of the illness haunting their family until it was too late. She didn't know if it had been a blessing or a curse to test positive for the same gene when she'd been young, having lived the rest of her life fearing the same fate as her sibling. Her mother too had feared for her, never wanting her to take part in anything too strenuous or stressful, leading to a somewhat isolated existence.

Although losing her mother too before she'd fully entered into adulthood had been traumatic, it had given her the independence to go to university, to train for a job where she could help others.

Her own diagnosis had come five years ago when she'd begun to experience some symptoms of having the same condition— fatigue, swelling in her ankles and belly. It had almost been a relief when her suspicions had been confirmed after spending her whole life waiting for them to appear, so she could deal with them instead of simply worrying what might happen.

For now, her symptoms were under control with medication, but if they worsened she might need a pacemaker to deliver electrical impulses to regulate her heartbeat. The worst scenario would be if she needed a heart transplant should a pacing device and medication fail to work, and that thought was always at the back of her mind.

It was probably why it was so important for her to make a difference for as long as she could, and why one unnecessary loss was too many.

The sound of sirens and the sight of flashing blue lights blazed through the twilight gloom as a fire engine from the local station raced by. Hopefully they would get there in time to save whoever was in trouble.

The two incidents were uppermost in her mind as she made the short walk back across the beach to her small bungalow, population one, ever since her diagnosis. Relationships had never been easy for a woman who insisted she never wanted children. There had been a few partners who had professed to the same thinking, only to later change their minds as time wore on and they were faced with their own mortality. For her, it seemed selfish to bring another generation into this world, only to pass on the same death sentence her father had unwittingly given her and her sister.

The knowledge of the condition was both a blessing and a curse. Her parents had been able to live their lives freely until illness interrupted it. Lily had been hyperaware of that same illness from an early age and it had affected all of her life decisions. Her career, her relationships and her future were all based around the medical condition and it was the reason she was alone. With no family or significant other to mourn her, she would never leave anyone as devastated as she and her mother had been by loss.

She would do everything in her power for the wider community to avoid that same heartache too.

Charlie 'Finn' Finnegan heard the click-clack of heels long before he spotted the woman who had recently become a royal pain in his backside. This was the first time they had actually met in person but, judging by the phone conversations and email exchanges, they were in for a major personality clash. The local community centre had been commandeered especially for this mediation meeting, all departments keen for them to set aside their differences and co-operate on the matter. It seemed pointless when she had already gone above his head to the Fire Service Group Commander to get the green light for her harebrained scheme after he had raised objections. Nevertheless, he would fight his corner for the sake of his team.

Lily Riordan couldn't have been more than five foot two—a good foot shorter than him—but she seemed to project a much bigger personality. Wearing a figure-hugging royal blue dress which matched her eyes, she exuded confidence. Her loose honey-blonde curls danced on her shoulders with every step and her full red lips were drawn into a tight line, looking as though she was preparing to go into battle. Finn couldn't help but smile when he saw her.

'It's nice to meet you, Ms Riordan.'

Although she shook his outstretched hand she didn't look any happier about this than he was. 'I wish it was in more congenial circumstances. I don't believe in wasting anybody's time, Mr Finnegan, including my own.'

She clearly wasn't one to suffer fools gladly and he already liked that about her.

A person who wore their heart on their sleeve was easier to deal with than someone who hid what they were really thinking.

His mind flitted briefly to the dark memories he tried not to revisit too often. Of his wife asleep, or so he'd thought, until he couldn't wake her. He'd known she was tired, having trouble sleeping, but she hadn't confided in him about how much she was struggling with her workload at the hospital. If he had known he would have kept a closer eye on her, monitored the medication she had been secretly taking. Although he would never know if the overdose had been an accident or not, he liked to think she would never purposely have left him and their girls. Instead, he preferred to imagine she'd simply been so tired she had mistakenly taken more than the prescribed dose of sleeping tablets. Either way, the loss had left him devastated and with the guilt of failing his family. To have someone unafraid to tell him exactly what she thought was refreshing and Finn appreciated it.

'I appreciate that, but do call me Finn. Now, shall we?' He stood back to let her enter the room first, with their mediator following behind.

They took their seats on either side of the large table, with the mediator at the head. Leaving them no choice but to face each other. Lily leaned across the table, hands clasped, ready to do business.

'Now, my name is Joe Mussen, and we're here tonight to discuss the involvement of the local fire service in a new cardiac care initiative and resolve any issues or concerns so we can press ahead.' The mediator took out his notes from his bag and set them on the table. Finn wondered if he should have put his thoughts in writing, but Lily didn't seem to have a list of statistics or facts to bamboozle him with. This apparently was just a discussion to iron out any wrinkles, when the hospital board and the fire service had already decided this was going ahead.

Finn did not want to be responsible for overworked, stressed members of his team when he knew how that could end up. If someone had stepped in for his wife, seeing the adverse effect the extra hours and responsibility was taking on her, his life would be very different.

'So, *Finn*, as local watch commander, the hospital board would prefer to have your co-operation.'

He noted she did not include herself in that statement.

'I don't see why, when it's going ahead with or without my approval.' It had been made apparent to him that he would not have the final say on the matter and, with the good press the scheme was going to generate, his opposition was in the minority.

'That may be so, but they want you involved.'

'Ah yes, the face of the campaign,' he sneered. For some reason the department had deemed him the most suitable for the job. Apparently he would add some gravitas to the campaign or some such nonsense. It was probably the greying hair. There were much younger, more attractive men on the crew than him who would have jumped at the chance. He would rather not have been involved at all but even he had orders to follow. It didn't mean he had to be gracious about it.

Lily raised an eyebrow. 'I don't know about that, but as commander it would look odd if you weren't there for the launch. I will be representing the hospital.'

'It was your idea...' He'd be surprised if she let anyone else take the credit for something she was obviously very passionate about. Finn couldn't fault her for that, but he couldn't agree with her plans. Not at the possible expense of his crew's mental health.

'My idea, yes, but I'm also the lead cardiologist. You hold the most senior position locally too. They want us both present for the public launch.'

'On Valentine's Day, I'm led to believe. Don't you think that's a bit corny?' He hated the commercialism of the day anyway, but now that he didn't have his wife to celebrate it with he would have preferred to treat it as any other day. Instead, he was supposed to join in some elaborate publicity campaign, no doubt littered with hearts and flowers, to promote this enterprise.

Lily had the decency to blush, her pale complexion taking on an attractive rosy hue. 'That wasn't my idea, but I understand the board wants as much public awareness as possible. The premise of providing emergency cardiac care does tie in with the day, I suppose. Look, I have no desire to be paraded in front of the cameras either, but it's for the greater good.'

He scoffed at that. 'For the greater good' implied someone else had to make a sacrifice. In the past, his wife had been one of many nurses who had given up time with their families to take on extra shifts and look after the sick. She had undoubtedly saved more lives with her selfless attitude, but it had ultimately cost her and her family everything. He did not want the men he worked alongside to make the same sacrifice.

The mediator, who had been silently taking in all they had to say until now, coughed. 'Perhaps we should focus on the reservations you have, Mr Finnegan, and address those one by one.'

Lily cocked her head to one side, waiting for him to begin and listening, a smug smile spreading across her lips. As though she was merely humouring him.

'First, and most importantly of all, my

crew are not medical professionals. Asking them to attend emergency cardiac cases goes beyond the remit of our jobs.'

'We have fire crew with first aid training and defibrillators in local access points. My suggestion is to combine the two. In instances where cardiac patients aren't going to be reached quickly enough by paramedics, we could equip your team to attend and treat emergencies. It could make all the difference between someone living and dying if they're treated before they get to me at the hospital.'

'I appreciate that. However, I have to consider the welfare of my crew. Isn't this opening them up to all sorts of law suits if something goes wrong? It's an extra responsibility none of us signed on for. Which I have repeatedly pointed out to you.' It had been his first reaction to oppose the scheme for this very reason and it still was when he was the one tasked with looking after his crew.

'And, as I have told you on several occasions, they will be given full training in the use of a defibrillator. All that is expected of them is to follow the instructions on the use of the machines. We will also provide additional assistance over the phone until paramedics are in attendance and able to take over. We're not expecting miracles, Mr… Finn. Just a little extra time, which can make all the difference in cardiac care. I understand your concerns, but we are talking about saving people's lives here. I'm sure we can find some way of safeguarding your crew.'

'I'm sorry, but that's not good enough. It will put extra stress on my men, along with the additional hours involved. I admire your dedication to your job and patients but they're not my responsibility.' Finn had enough on his plate with work and raising his two young daughters without the added stress of Ms Riordan breathing down his neck.

'Ms Riordan, can you offer any further support to Mr Finnegan's team from the cardiology department? It could help to have a member of your team available, at least until the scheme is up and running.' The mediator, who had been watching their verbal tennis match across the table until now, spoke up with a suggestion which seemed neither of them could really object to. Much to Finn's annoyance.

'If I, or one of my colleagues are available we could attend the first callouts too. I'll do whatever it takes to make this work.' Lily, of course, jumped in to offer her personal assistance, leaving Finn floundering and grasping for other reasons to object.

'What about the extra work involved? I assume this is a voluntary scheme?' Although he hadn't volunteered his services, it seemed he would be the one to coordinate it all.

'It will be, but I intended it to run alongside your regular shifts.'

'I can't afford for my crew to be caught up elsewhere if a shout comes in.' That meant leaving them vulnerable in two areas and that wasn't going to work for any of them.

'Perhaps we could have one person per shift with a response vehicle dedicated to emergency medical calls, liaising with the hospital team.'

'That's a lot of responsibility for one person and it means I'm a team member down every shift.'

Lily sighed, letting him know she was exasperated with the hurdles he kept putting in her way, but this was what this meeting was for—to find solutions.

'You could put it to your crew and see what they think. I'm sure you will have volunteers. You might even be able to do it yourself.' She was goading him, unaware that he had taken more of a back seat role these days in his new position as watch commander.

It was his job to co-ordinate response to large scale incidents and, rather than the adrenaline rush of running into fires, he got his buzz making sure everyone stayed safe and did their own jobs well. One way he'd been able to reassure his daughters they weren't going to lose him too.

If anyone was going to dedicate themselves to this new position it made sense it would be him, but that would entail working closely with Miss Riordan on a regular basis and he wasn't sure either of them would survive that. One wrong move and he knew she would rip him apart. The thought did nothing to garner his support for her cause.

For two people who were virtual strangers, they'd seemed to get under each other's skin very quickly. It was as intriguing as it was frustrating to Finn, who was used to being the one in charge of everything. Including his emotions.

'Of course.'

Just as they appeared to be making progress, with Finn realising he was fighting a losing battle, the mediator gripped the edge of the table, head bowed, sweat breaking out over his forehead.

'Are you okay?' Lily was first on her feet to check on him. He stumbled and Finn got out of his chair to go and support him.

'Perhaps you should sit down. I'll get you a glass of water.'

'I'll be fine. I just felt a little woozy.'

'You look a bit pale. Finn's right, I think you should take a seat and maybe loosen your tie.' Lily did her best to convince the mediator to take their advice but he shook them both off.

'I'll be fine,' he insisted and shooed them back to their own seats.

Finn and Lily reluctantly backed away and took their positions on either side of the table again, their gaze never leaving the clearly ailing man, who was dabbing his forehead with a handkerchief.

'Now, where were we?' He shuffled through his papers, then suddenly grabbed his left arm and crumpled to the floor.

'Men are so damn stubborn when it comes to their health,' Lily complained, though she was rushing to help.

'That's why we need people looking out for us. Just as I'm doing with my crew.' He used the moment to reiterate the reason he'd gone to war in the first place. They were both simply trying to do the right thing by others.

'Hmph.' She huffed out a breath as she knelt down beside the prostrate figure of the man who had been sent to corral them. Finn hoped they weren't the cause of his sudden illness.

'Joe? Can you hear me? Finn, he's not breathing.' Lily had already loosened his tie and opened the top button on the man's shirt.

'I think I saw a defibrillator on the wall outside. I'll get it if you can start chest compressions?' He trusted Lily knew what she was doing in that department and he bolted out to get the medical equipment needed to save this stranger's life, calling an ambulance from his mobile phone on the way.

By the time he came back she was pumping the man's chest and counting every compression. 'No response. I need you to follow the instructions on the defibrillator so we can try and get his heart restarted.'

Finn nodded. He had basic first aid training but this was the first time he'd actually had to use one of these machines. It seemed relatively straightforward and once he had undone their patient's shirt he was able to adhere the sticky pads to the skin.

The defibrillator provided vocal instructions for each step and Lily and Finn had to stand back as the electric shocks were delivered to the heart. After each one, Lily checked again for a pulse until eventually they could both see his chest begin to rise and fall.

'Joe? It's Lily. Can you open your eyes for me? Finn, we need to get him into the recovery position until the ambulance gets here,' Lily directed.

After disconnecting the defibrillator, Finn assisted in moving the patient onto his side.

Once they were sure he was no longer in immediate danger, they were both able to relax a little but remained on the floor with their backs against the wall, watching over the mediator they'd apparently driven to cardiac arrest.

'I'm going to phone the ambulance again. They should have been here by now.'

Lily gave him a half smile. 'Do you see now how important the response time is for cardiac patients? If we hadn't been here, or had the means to shock his heart, he wouldn't have made it.'

He couldn't argue with the facts and, without time to consider what he was doing, Finn had been part of saving the man's life. When it came down to it he knew that was the thought uppermost in both of their minds and if he had to do it again he would. The burden of responsibility or culpability had not come into the equation and they had both acted purely on instinct. Something he knew the rest of his crew would have done in the same circumstances.

'Okay. You've made your point. Although I think causing a man to have a heart attack

just to get your own way was going too far.'
He couldn't resist one more tease and was
rewarded with an exaggerated sigh for his
efforts.

This man would be the death of her. Lily had
never met anyone who seemed to enjoy an-
tagonising her so much, or she let bother her
so much. Usually, she did not waste energy
on people who apparently brought nothing
but trouble to her door. If her time on this
earth was limited she didn't want to have it
taken up with toxic relationships. She was
sure they could even have got this project
off the ground without Finn's compliance but
he pushed her buttons so hard she was determined to show him it would work and get
one up on him.

'So, have you had a change of heart? No
pun intended.' She afforded him a smile since
he had done so much to assist her. Whilst she
was used to these sudden life-or-death situations, it was probably new to him. At least
outside of his work environment. If he had
stuck to his belief that non-medical professionals should not get involved in a cardiac

emergency, it would have made things very difficult for her. However, Finn hadn't taken time to consider the consequences, acting on pure instinct to help. Exactly what she had been counting on by including another emergency service in attendance on cardiac calls.

Finn smiled back, and for the first time she noticed how blue his eyes were, now they weren't narrowed at her. The man was fit for his age, in all senses of the word. She guessed him to be in his late forties, his dark blond hair flecked with strands of barely noticeable silver. Yes, he was a handsome man, undoubtedly with a line of women who swooned at his stubborn macho persona, but she wasn't easily swayed by good looks.

It was his willingness to help tonight, despite his reservations, that made her see him in a different light. Though doing so was a futile exercise. If she was ever going to have one last fling, it would be with someone passing through town who she would hopefully never see again, to avoid hurt on either side.

'I'm willing to work together if you are.'

It wasn't a definitive answer to her question but sufficient to get the project up and running at least. Whether they could work together without causing further ructions remained to be seen.

CHAPTER TWO

'IS THIS REALLY NECESSARY?' Lily batted away the heart-shaped helium balloons lining her path but managed to walk straight into the red and pink streamers hanging from the ceiling.

'I think they're keen to reiterate the purpose of this scheme. That it's for heart patients only and shouldn't be abused by those hoping for a lift to hospital appointments or who want us to pop round with a takeaway. Plus it's Valentine's Day so, you know...' Finn's soft voice in her ear caused the hairs on the back of her neck to stand to attention when he was so close she could feel his breath on her skin.

'Oh, I know. Let's bring in all the clichés we can to hammer the point home.' She rolled her eyes. Being deceived by the idea of love and romance wasn't an affliction she suffered from. She left it to naïve young couples who had for ever to fool themselves into thinking it could solve everything. Life, and death, had taught her it only complicated things and made life so much harder. All the people she had ever loved had died and, as for romance, it had brought nothing but heartache when she couldn't give her partners what they needed—children and time.

'Something tells me you didn't get any cards in the post.'

'And I suppose you did?'

'Two, actually.'

More eye-rolling. Not only was he handsome but he knew it. One of the worst traits a man could have.

'Let me guess, one came from a grateful young woman who found herself locked out of her house in nothing but a towel and you came to the rescue? And the other…some impressionable schoolgirl whose class had a tour of the fire station?' Boasting about how many cards he'd received was juvenile, and clearly mentioned to get a rise out of her. He had, of course, succeeded.

Finn laughed so hard she actually felt the vibration through to her very bones. 'Actually, they were from my daughters, but it's good to know what you really think about me. You'll have to take my word for it that I'm not a ladies' man who would take advantage of vulnerable females.'

Lily wished the ceiling would collapse and bury her under the hearts and flowers they were surrounded by for the press call. He pulled his phone from his pocket and proceeded to deepen her embarrassment by showing her pictures of the adorable handmade cards his girls had made. Judging by the handwriting and childish representation of hearts, they were from his very young offspring. She could also see the wedding ring shining on his hand now.

'I'm so sorry. I didn't realise you were married with children. That's so lovely. You must be very proud.' She had taken something so sweet and turned it into something tawdry. When she was around him she apparently had no filter and said things before she had time to think about it.

'Widowed with children,' he corrected,

scrolling through to show her a picture of two gorgeous little blonde cherubs.

Lily's blood froze in her veins at hearing his statement. It had never occurred to her that Finn had gone through something so tragic, and it went some way to explaining his initial reluctance in getting involved. His concerns about the extra time involved, as well as the added responsibility, made sense when he was looking after two young girls who had lost their mother. It made the whole matter more tragic and her heart went out to him and the two little ones left behind in their grief.

'I'm so sorry. I had no idea. Thank you again for agreeing to all of this. I know you must have your work cut out for you already, juggling work and parenthood.' Especially on this particular day, which was likely hard for him anyway as a widower. She didn't know how long it had been since he'd lost his wife, or the circumstances, but she certainly could empathise with the devastation it caused in one's life to lose a loved one.

That he was even able to function was amazing to her, never mind working in such a demanding job and now taking on this new role she'd helped rope him into. Yes, guilt was beginning to poison her feel-good endorphins about setting this whole thing up now she was aware of Finn's circumstances. Would she have backed off if she'd known? Probably not, but she might have been a little more understanding and less confrontational. She knew how his little girls would be feeling—lost, lonely and terrified that they were going to lose everyone they loved. It must have been extremely difficult for Finn to return to his line of work, facing those life-or-death situations every day while promising his daughters he wouldn't leave them too. Lily's heart went out to all of them.

However, Finn simply shrugged, seeming to take it all in his stride. Probably because he had no other option than to carry on with life for the sake of his children. 'My mum helps out with the babysitting, but I just have to get on with things. Try to keep things as normal as possible for them.'

There was a softer side to him when he talked about his family and Lily could see why he hadn't mentioned them before. It was private and a deeply personal matter. One he had chosen to share with her today and she was privileged to have seen beneath that hard, unyielding surface she'd encountered on their first meeting. They both had their reasons for being guarded, but she wasn't ready to share hers just yet. If ever.

'Okay, guys, if you could scooch up closer so I can *try* and fit you both in the same picture, it would be really great.'

'And if you could talk to us with a little respect it would be really great too,' Finn chastised the patronising young photographer rolling his eyes at them. The few words spoken in a measured, firm tone was enough to fluster both the employee of the national newspaper and Lily.

Since hitting her forties it seemed to her she had become invisible to the younger generation and at other times spoken to as though she had lost her faculties. With her credibility as a cardiologist not immediately apparent to strangers, it appeared to her she was judged by the crinkles at her eyes and dress size and found unworthy of interest for today's image-obsessed millennials. She wasn't able to do as much strenuous exercise as she used to in case she aggravated her condition and that, along with the swelling it caused in various parts of her body, meant she wasn't as svelte as she had been.

Pearce had pointed it out numerous times. That was just one of the reasons he was now her ex. Curvy, it seemed, wasn't what all men appreciated in a partner. No matter if it was caused by a medical condition or a fondness for cake. In her case, likely both.

It was difficult to stay buoyed in a world where looks were valued above experience and credentials. A world where even a man such as Charlie Finnegan was dismissed as an 'oldie' and therefore not worthy of respect, despite his service and dedication to the community. Not forgetting how good he looked in his uniform.

He wasn't wearing the whole outfit today, of course, but the smart white shirt and tie ensemble was still hot. It was a uniform of sorts and he exuded authority. Lily hopefully had a while to go before menopause struck but she still had eyes and Finn managed to inspire a hot flush creeping over her skin which took her completely unawares.

It was inconvenient to find him attractive, not only because they were working together but also because he had so much personal baggage. However, it was also a reminder that she wasn't dead yet at least.

'The article will be in tomorrow's paper,' the photographer mumbled before he shuffled off out of sight.

They'd already given an interview to the reporter, recounting the details of the new scheme. Now all they had to do was repeat it all for the evening regional news. They were using the same backdrop for the item, much to her and Finn's chagrin.

'All of this pink and red décor is starting to make me feel queasy,' he whispered as the bubbly TV reporter moved in for her turn at the questioning.

'I know what you mean. It's a bit overkill, but I suppose it'll make for good TV.' Syncing the launch with Valentine's Day gave the press an angle to work with and it was a nice piece to end the usual doom and gloom news roundup.

She heard the rumble of Finn's stomach, followed by a chuckle.

'Sorry. It's been a long day without much of a break for me.'

'Not to worry. This shouldn't take long,' the reporter assured them, beaming. A familiar face on the local television, the pretty young blonde was also much friendlier than the photographer who had preceded her.

Lily and Finn were fitted with their microphone packs and waited as the crew set up the camera and sound equipment around them.

'The worst of it is all the restaurants will be crammed full of loved-up couples and the menu will be twice the price.' She was a tad cynical when it came to love these days. It had eluded her. Or, rather, she had dodged it when it presented itself. In her case it seemed a wasted exercise when she might pop her clogs at any given second.

'All courses with poncy titles like Cupid's Charcuterie and Passion Parfait,' Finn added.

'Served with the lighting down low enough so you can't see the inflated prices on the menu.'

'So cynical. I'm a widower, what's your excuse?'

'Experience.' Let him think she was still a woman about town with admirers who took her out to restaurants on the most expensive night of the year instead of a spinster who would rather cook herself a steak and sit in front of the telly with a glass of wine than be in that cattle market again. Life was too short not to enjoy the things which did give her pleasure and avoid those which didn't. Okay, so she was well past her prime even without the doomed family medical history, but a woman still liked a man to think she was desirable to others even if it was fantasy.

'If you'd like, I could make us something to eat back at the station. I'll be taking the first shift overseeing our new venture and I could show you around?'

The offer of both having a meal cooked for her and seeing around the fire station, on Valentine's Day no less, was a pleasant surprise. Usually she spent the evening on her own, mourning the love life she never had with the help of a bottle of red wine and copious amounts of chocolate.

'That would be lovely, thank you.'

It would be churlish of her to decline simply to save face. He knew she had no one interested in her romantically and there was no need to pretend she might have something else lined up for the night. Besides, she was keen to check out the fire station and Finn's cooking skills.

After his initial opposition, he had been making an effort to set hostilities aside. They seemed to have bonded today over their joint cynicism over the commercialisation of February the fourteenth, and he'd backed her against an obnoxious photographer. She owed him and a thaw in relations would be best if they were going to be working together to make this scheme a success.

They did their bit for the TV cameras and answered all the questions, making the information about their joint enterprise as clear as possible for the general public. By the end of the publicity drive, Lily was emotionally and physically drained but also hungry.

'Are you ready to head to the station to sample my delights?' Finn waggled his eyebrows at her and made her laugh.

'Yes, please.' She'd be glad to get out of this heart-fest and relax. Okay, she would've preferred to go home and change first, but she had to remind herself this wasn't a date and it shouldn't matter that she didn't have time to retouch her make-up or put on a clean outfit. They would both have to make do with the navy business suit and white blouse she'd put on first thing this morning. Although changing out of her heels would've been a nice way to wind down, she would have to suffer a little longer.

'Do you need a lift?' Finn stood back and let her walk ahead of him out of the building. As she walked past she was sure she caught the scent of smoke and sweat mixed with soap. Apparently that was her new kink as she found herself inhaling another lungful before realising she hadn't answered his question.

'No, it's fine. I've got my car here.' Thank goodness. If she'd been enclosed in such a small space with him she might have ended up sniffing him like some sort of weirdo.

'I'm guessing you know the way, so I'll see you there.' He left her in the car park smiling like a loon and wondering what the hell was wrong with her.

Finn didn't know how he'd ended up here at the station cooking dinner for this woman when they'd needed a mediator not so long ago. He supposed so much had happened in that short space of time it had left them both reeling. Starting this new work collaboration, doing publicity, not to mention working together to save a man's life had brought them closer in a way he was sure neither of them could have anticipated.

Perhaps it was being of a similar age, relationship status and career path, helping others, which had finally bonded them together but it had become important somewhere along the line that neither of them should be alone tonight. Not that she would have thanked him for it, he was sure. Lily struck him as someone very confident and capable of being on her own. Yet the way the young photographer had spoken to her earlier had angered him almost as much as how easily she had accepted it. Dinner had been a gesture of friendship, an olive branch, and hopefully a foundation for a good working relationship between their departments.

He was also glad the rest of the guys were out on a shout so he didn't have to answer awkward questions about why he was entertaining a woman on site.

'How do you like your steak?' He'd stopped into the high-end butcher's outside of town so he could offer her something more than a microwave meal or a takeaway, which was sometimes all he felt like making himself at the end of the day. When he was off with the girls he cooked healthy meals and on his shifts here he often made dinner for the rest of the crew. Sometimes, however, cooking for one seemed too much hassle. It had been a long time since he'd shared dinner for two.

'Well done and no comments about how it ruins the steak et cetera. I like it how I like it, and that's preferably without the sight of blood.'

He held his hands up. 'No judgement here. Although I do prefer mine with a little more juice…and flavour.'

Finn ducked from the tea towel which Lily flung at him. She had insisted on helping in the kitchen, even if that only extended to washing and drying the dishes the other guys had left in a hurry and swatting him for making jokes at her expense.

The staff canteen wasn't the most glamorous setting, but this wasn't a date and they'd had enough hearts and flowers for one day. This was simply a shared meal between two people who'd had a busy day and were hungry. It didn't hurt that Lily was good company. He enjoyed teasing her, watching the tiger claw back and give as good as she got. The only females he spent time with these days were his daughters, his mother and those he encountered at work, often too traumatised to hold a conversation.

'Do you bring women back here often?' Lily teased, as though following his train of thought. 'You must get a lot of interest in your fireman's pole.'

Finn paused in the middle of dishing up to raise an eyebrow at her. It was quite the innuendo to chuck into the conversation at the start of their meal.

Her cheeks flushed that adorable shade of pink again before she narrowed her eyes at him. 'You know what I mean, Finn. No need to get smutty.'

'Hey, I'm not the one talking dirty,' he said with a smirk, setting the heaped plates of steak, chips and salad onto the table under the fluorescent lights.

'I'm sure you're used to it,' she bit back without hesitation. It was true, in an all-male environment conversation got bawdy at times. Finn didn't participate but neither did he take offence when it was all part of the humour which helped them deal with the darker nature of their work.

'I'll admit we do get the odd lonely woman, and man, who gets us out under false pretences. Not to mention the drop-ins we get from people who just like to have a nosy around. I think it's something to do with the uniform.' He shook his head. It never ceased to amaze him what got people hot under the collar.

'I think it's everything to do with the uniform,' Lily muttered as she took her first bite of steak.

It took Finn by surprise that she might be turned on by anything so shallow as appearance. Lily Riordan struck him as someone who would've needed a lot more to impress her than a helmet and a bib and braces.

There was something in that realisation that she was as human as anyone else when it came to physical attraction which piqued his interest. Something he had no intention of exploring. He was only flesh and blood and there were certain physical attributes in a woman he appreciated, all of which Lily encompassed now he thought about it, but since his wife's death he had tried to put those thoughts to the back of his mind. Being attracted to another woman still seemed like a betrayal, even a year on.

'I know some of the younger single guys are happy with the benefits that the stereotypical romantic view of our job brings with it, but I'm not interested. Since my wife died, you're the only woman I've brought here and this is a celebratory dinner for our joint enterprise only.'

He stabbed his slightly bloody steak with his fork and sawed it enthusiastically with his knife. The sooner this was over and they retreated back to their respective departments, the better. He didn't want anyone getting the wrong idea that he was somehow getting back into the market and actively looking for a replacement for Sara. That wasn't going to happen any time soon, if ever, when his daughters were his priority.

'Well, that's me told,' she muttered and took a sip from her glass of water before they both lapsed into an awkward silence, interrupted only by the sound of two people trying to finish their meal as quickly as possible.

Finn was almost glad when the raucous arrival of his colleagues crashed in around them. Almost. When the loud chatter of the men returning reached the canteen door then stopped abruptly as they took in the scene before them, he knew he had some explaining to do.

It was like a farce as the guys stopped abruptly in the doorway, tripping those behind as they stared agog at Lily. She too froze, fork full of steak and salad hovering in the air, as she turned and looked at Finn, waiting for him to say something. He had no idea why he felt embarrassed and guilty. It wasn't as though he had just been sprung making out with her in one of the dorm beds. Even if he had been, they were two grown adults and whether they were having sex or sharing an awkward dinner, it was no one else's business.

'Lads, this is Lily Riordan. The cardiologist who introduced the new defib scheme for us to trial.' He was sure some of the men had probably seen her during the course of the set-up but he thought he should clarify who she was, even if he couldn't explain why she was here now eating dinner with him.

'Ah, right. Nice to meet you.'

'Hi. Any more of those steaks going?'

'Give us a few of your chips, Finn.'

The introduction appeared sufficient to end the stare-off as the men unfroze and invaded the canteen, helping themselves to his fries as they passed by. Lily nodded a hello before returning to her meal. He had lost his appetite since their arrival. There was something about real life disturbing the moment which had brought some unexpected emotions. Primarily guilt. As though simply being seen with another woman, enjoying her company, was something he should be ashamed about as a widower.

'I think there are some sausages in the fridge. I could stick those in the oven and do the rest of the chips for you, if you'd like?' He got up, glad to have a reason to leave the table.

'Cheers.'

'Has the chief has given you a tour of the place?' A couple of the men sat down beside Lily, unperturbed by the scene now they knew why she was here.

'No, he hasn't.'

'I'm sure Ms Riordan has better things to do than look at the mess you lot have left behind.' He'd shared enough with her here tonight, and showing her around behind the scenes at his place of work, where he lived and slept during his shifts away from home, now seemed too intimate.

'I thought you might want me to stick around in case a call came in, for emergency medical support?' She frowned and he could sense her confusion when that was exactly what they were supposed to be doing. Except being around Lily any longer suddenly seemed dangerous to his equilibrium and the life he had been living for the past year.

'It's probably not necessary. I mean I've done the training and the odds of getting a call on our first night are slim.' He positioned himself out in the kitchen, keeping the wooden counter as a physical barrier between them.

'I'm sure you're right.' Lily set down her cutlery and got to her feet, leaving the others to scavenge the leftovers on both of their plates. There was something in her tone which made Finn regret the abrupt end he had brought to their meal. A pained fragility he hadn't expected Lily to possess and that he could have done without being party to.

CHAPTER THREE

'WE CAN CANCEL if you'd prefer? It is only a courtesy catch-up after all.' Lily was letting Finn off the hook. They had arranged to have an informal monthly meeting to discuss how the project was going, but that was before the awkward dinner they'd shared at the fire station. She hadn't heard from him until tonight, an hour before they were supposed to meet, when he'd called to say he couldn't get away. After the last time they had been together she would be only too glad if she never had to see him again.

The way he'd reacted when his crew had come back during their meal had made her feel about two inches high and she didn't need to be around anyone embarrassed to be seen with her. Life was too short to spend with toxic people and the change in his demeanour had been too obvious to ignore when their dinner had been gatecrashed. It didn't matter that there hadn't been anything going on other than companionship and bonding after their day with the press, she had seen the shame on his face when his colleagues had suspected more.

Her weight or her size didn't generally bother her when she had so much more to worry about—what was going on inside her body. It didn't make his reaction any less disappointing. After seeing him stand up to the patronising young photographer, she had expected more of Charlie Finnegan. That her achievements, her good heart and maybe even her personality meant more to him than carrying a few extra pounds. Although it had apparently been enough for Pearce to stop fancying her. That had been no great loss but she had put more stock in Finn.

If her appearance was all that mattered to him she was sure any business they had to discuss in the future could be done via email or text from now on. Then perhaps she wouldn't let her mind wander where it shouldn't, thinking there was a mutual attraction going on and not simply her appreciation of a fine-looking man. Perhaps that was bothering her more than the idea that curvy women weren't his thing. That she'd mistakenly believed there'd been a spark between them when it was nothing more than wishful thinking.

A lucky escape, she supposed, because Finn was never going to be a safe option for her. He wasn't someone she could ever consider for her casual type of relationships, which burned brightly for a while before she let them fizzle out so she could move on with no regrets or broken hearts. Pearce had upset her with his comments about her putting on weight, but she hadn't loved him enough to cry herself to sleep at night when they'd broken up. She was always careful not to get too involved when she couldn't promise anyone for ever.

Finn was different. He was grieving and he had two little girls to look after. Complications she certainly didn't need in her life. This was an attraction she would simply have to let fade away if she wanted to avoid any emotional fallout.

'No, I have a few issues I want to sort out. There are a couple of teething problems I'd like to talk to you about. Maeve, can you give your sister her doll back, please? No, I don't think she would look better with a haircut...' His voice trailed off as he apparently addressed his daughter in the background. Lily could almost picture the scene and though she was amused at first at the thought of him trying to wrangle two warring tots, her smile soon turned into a frown at the thought he might pass on his superficial judgement on the female body to another generation. She definitely shouldn't be thinking how sweet it was to hear him with his girls either when that was trouble waiting to happen.

'If this is a bad time you can just jot down a few points you want me to look at and pop them in an email.' Then she could end this call and hopefully never have to talk to him again.

'No, I'd rather talk in person. Though I'm having babysitter issues tonight. My mum was supposed to have the girls but she's down with a migraine. I'm merely suggesting a change of venue from the community centre, if you don't mind having two extra distractions? I'll try to get them to sleep before you come over but I can't promise they won't get out of bed again with a thousand and one questions about who you are.'

'Are you sure you'll be okay with that?' She couldn't resist a little dig since the last time he'd had to introduce her to anyone he'd almost died of embarrassment.

'Of course. I'll text you directions and I guess we'll see you soon.' He hung up without giving her any further chance to back out of the meeting now there was a change of venue. She was curious about what was going on when he was inviting her into his inner sanctum after seemingly regretting inviting her into his workplace. It was the only reason why she was grabbing her coat and bag and heading out of the door to make the meeting when she'd told herself any involvement in his personal life was a mistake.

Deep down she knew she was hoping for an explanation for his previous behaviour so she could stop cursing his name. Okay, so it had bothered her a lot that he found the idea abhorrent that anyone could believe they were together romantically, because she so desperately wanted to be wrong about the kind of man Charlie Finnegan was. If he wasn't the shallow Neanderthal she had believed him to be when she'd walked out of the station that night, she knew she was in real trouble.

Because she wanted to like him. Because it had hurt so damn much when he had publicly rejected her. Because she knew she was already ignoring all the warning signs which would normally send her running in the opposite direction.

Finn was a terrible liar. There was nothing about the project that he urgently needed to talk to Lily about or that couldn't wait for the next time he saw her. So far they'd dealt with a couple of emergency calls, both times able to restart the patients' hearts until the paramedics arrived and took over.

It was his conscience which had been bothering him where Lily was concerned.

Looking back on that night at the station, he could see he'd been incredibly rude. He'd invited her back for a meal then acted as though he couldn't get rid of her fast enough when the boys came in. He wanted to explain, and apologise. Then perhaps he could stop replaying that day together in his head over and over again.

The stuff about not being able to get a babysitter was true though. If he cancelled at such short notice now it wasn't going to help her see him in a better light, it would merely confirm the idea he was flaky and untrustworthy. Something which would not sit well with him in his position in the community. He needed people to trust him, especially those he worked alongside.

Although he would have preferred not to do this at his place with the girls there. They were impressionable and he never brought anyone home, let alone a woman. He didn't want them to get any ideas about who she was or how important she might be in his life. Hopefully he would have them settled in bed before she got here and they would never have to cross paths. Thus still managing to keep his home life and work life separate.

'Teeth brushed, girls.' Finn hustled the

two pyjama-clad munchkins towards the bathroom.

'Who were you talking to on the phone, Dada?' The littlest Finnegan also had the biggest ears.

'It was someone from work.' He kicked over the little wooden stool they used for her to reach the sink with her sister and squeezed some toothpaste onto the waiting toothbrushes.

'Is someone coming over, Daddy?' Now she had piqued her sister Niamh's interest, her eyes shining bright with undisguised delight at the prospect of having a visitor in the house. Clearly it had been too long since they'd had company other than their grandmother.

'Uh…just a lady who works at the hospital. I need you girls in bed so we can talk.' He didn't want to lie to his daughters, especially if there was going to be a stranger coming to the house, but he knew this would seem like a big deal to them.

His suspicions were confirmed as his eldest halted brushing her teeth to look at him, toothpaste dribbling down her chin. 'A lady?'

Her astonishment made him smile.

'Yes, a real live lady is coming to the house, but only if good little girls are tucked up under the covers.' Finn grabbed both girls in a bear hug, blowing raspberries on their necks and making them squeal.

He'd taken this for granted when they were babies, working all hours and leaving bedtime rituals for his wife to manage. It was too late to get that time back but he was determined to be with them as much as he could. Not easy as a single parent working shifts, but he tried to be there for breakfasts and bedtimes together where it was possible. He'd moved closer to his mum to have some support when it seemed as though he and the girls would never be normal again. Hearing them laugh, being able to enjoy the simple things in life with his daughters again was a salve for the wound of losing his partner. It would never completely heal, but having his daughters eased the loneliness.

He and Sara had been best friends, childhood sweethearts, together since high school. Thinking they would have for ever together, they had waited until their careers were flourishing before starting a family. It had never occurred to either of them that he would be left alone to raise their daughters from such a young age. He hadn't been apart from Sara since the age of thirteen and living without her had been a struggle for all of them, settling into new routines whilst grieving.

The death of their mother was such a difficult thing for the girls to comprehend at their young age and though there had been plenty of tears and tantrums as they tried to adjust to their new lives, they were managing. It was important, therefore, that nothing disturb their fragile equilibrium. Including the girls getting the wrong idea about him having a female acquaintance at the house.

The doorbell rang and he cursed himself for getting them excitable when he should have been singing them to sleep with a lullaby or reading until they dropped off to sleep. Instead they were running around the house screaming, the pitch of which had risen with the added excitement of a visitor. He had no choice but to answer the door and introduce them to Lily or he would have no chance of ever getting them to settle.

'Shh, girls. Now, we don't want to scare my friend away, so best behaviour,' he warned as he unlatched the door.

The girls nodded enthusiastically, looking fit to burst with the effort of restraint. Once he was sure they weren't going to hurl themselves at Lily like little lemmings jumping off a cliff, he opened the door wide.

'Hi, come on in.'

'Well, hello there.' As Lily entered the hallway she bent down to say hello to the girls, appearing to make their night.

'Who are you?'

'What's your name?'

'Are you having a sleepover with Daddy?'

'Daddy has two pillows on his bed and Mummy isn't here no more.'

As usual, his daughters said exactly what was on their minds, drawing a look of sympathy first from Lily, before she smirked at him.

'Sorry. They have no filter,' he said, trying to hustle them back towards their room in vain as they remained rooted to the spot, waiting for their visitor to answer.

'It's fine. My name is Lily, I'm a friend of

your Dad's and no, I won't be staying over. I have a big bed with two pillows to go home to too.'

Little Maeve seemed to contemplate this news before asking, 'Do your girls have a daddy in heaven?'

A frown crinkled Lily's forehead at the question before evening out into a sad smile as she seemed to realise what she was being asked. 'I don't have any children or a husband. I live on my own.'

'Why?'

'I never got married or had babies.'

'Why?'

The question he was asked at least a hundred times a day was now directed at Lily on a loop and where he had to put up with the constant questioning, she didn't. Especially when it was in danger of being too personal and intrusive.

'That's enough, Maeve. It's none of our business.' It was a private matter and though he was curious about her circumstances, he knew what it was like to be put on the spot. These past twelve months had been difficult when people had asked after his wife or enquired about his love life and he'd had to explain what had happened. Information he would not usually have volunteered. Lily had come here under the impression it was to talk about work, not her relationship status.

Still, she didn't appear to take offence or get embarrassed by his inquisitive offspring. 'I just wasn't as lucky as your daddy.'

Lily was smiling, her answer enough to send his two finally skipping off to their room, but Finn had caught the flicker of pain in her eyes as she'd said it. He wouldn't be human if he didn't wonder why a woman like Lily Riordan hadn't settled down with a family of her own when she seemed sad about not doing so. She was attractive, funny, feisty and intelligent, a catch for anyone should she want them, and suddenly he wondered if her past was as tragic as his own.

'Say goodnight to Lily. It's bedtime.' He'd brought her over to apologise, not make her feel even more miserable.

'Aww. Can Lily read us a bedtime story?' His daughters were not about to give up spending time with their new visitor so easily.

'I'll read you a story, the same as I do every night.'

The girls pouted. 'We want Lily.'

'You'll have to make do with boring old Dad.' Finn did not want to get into a battle of wills in front of her, not least because he usually gave in to his daughters' pleas and it would do nothing for his credibility to be seen to cave as easily as he normally did.

'I don't mind reading them a story.' Lily shrugged, sealing her own fate as his two girls grabbed both of her hands and dragged her towards the bedroom.

'It might get them to go to sleep quicker,' she whispered out the side of her mouth, giving him the impression she didn't want this to happen any more than he did. That gave him some comfort. Lily didn't come across as someone who wanted to inveigle herself into his or his girls' lives at all, so perhaps having her in his home wouldn't be as disastrous as he imagined. He'd say what he had to and she could go back to her place. Conscience salved, working relations smoothed over, no harm done.

Finn followed, though he was aware his

presence was unimportant now the girls had a new storyteller to entertain them. For such a small gesture on Lily's part to agree to read to them, it was obviously having an impact, as the girls jumped into their beds without further complaint.

Thankfully these days the prolonged bedtime routine was more about getting extra time under the guise of more stories, requests for glasses of water and, of course, a sudden need for the toilet. For a long time they'd been plagued by nightmares and a fear of the dark, no doubt a manifestation of their grief and loss of their mother.

He'd spent many a night sleeping in the space between their beds, where Lily was sitting now on a pink princess bean bag. Some mornings he would wake to find they had both crawled into bed beside him, and on the nights he'd been on call they'd hardly slept at all, worried he wouldn't come home again. Like Mummy.

Then there were the nights he'd been so lonely, expecting to roll over and see Sara, only to find an empty space. Those were the times he was glad the girls needed him, because they were all that had kept him going. Now they were adjusting to life, learning to live without Sara, perhaps it was time for them all to begin socialising outside of their little bubble. One visitor really shouldn't cause such a commotion.

The girls were enraptured with Lily's storytelling, as was he. Not everyone was as patient with two excitable young children as she had been so far. As she read their favourite fairy tale, complete with character voices and actions, she really brought the story to life. Finn couldn't help but think about her earlier comment about not having children of her own, made all the more tragic by the fact she seemed like a natural mother figure.

Finn didn't know if she had siblings who'd provided her with nieces or nephews, only that she was comfortable being with youngsters. Tonight, that was making his life easier as well as entertaining for her audience.

'And they all lived happily ever after.' Lily closed the book, rolling her eyes at Finn as if to say she didn't believe that was possible any more than he did.

He'd had the loving wife and beautiful family, only to have a very unhappy ending.

'One more?'

'Please!'

'No.' He ignored their pleas, knowing they would keep Lily here captive all night if they could get away with it.

'Can Lily come back another night, Daddy?'

'Can Lily have a sleepover with us?'

Their tenacity was admirable, if exhausting.

'No, now go to sleep and let me and Lily talk in peace.'

They eventually gave up the fight and lay down so he could tuck them under the covers.

'Goodnight,' he said to each of them as he kissed their foreheads.

When he looked up he was sure he saw tears in Lily's eyes, reiterating the sense that being childless was not something she had willingly chosen.

Once they'd left the room and closed the door he let out a sigh. 'Sorry about that. They're not used to seeing anyone else here except my mother.'

'It's fine. They're lovely girls. Very inquisitive,' she said, chuckling.

'They're a handful all right.' Finn led the way back downstairs, heading to the kitchen for a much-needed caffeine hit. He switched the kettle on while Lily took a seat at the breakfast bar, the first face he had seen, other than his daughters', across there in over a year.

'It must have been really difficult for you, raising them on your own, but you've clearly done a good job.'

Lily's unexpected praise and understanding was something Finn didn't realise he needed until that moment and it wedged a lump of emotion in his throat. Since losing Sara he'd done his best to raise the girls the way they'd both wanted, having to take on both parenting roles. He hadn't always got it right, but hearing someone tell him he was doing well meant the world. Lily saw him, saw behind the tough chief façade to the grieving family man struggling as a single parent. She was probably the only one who did and that didn't sit comfortably with him. It made him feel vulnerable at a time when he needed to be stronger than ever for his family.

'I can't say it's been plain sailing, but we have no choice but to get on with things. I have to be Mum and Dad and it's taken me a while to get used to doing all the things Sara did while I was at work. Little things like braiding their hair suddenly seemed so important. I had to watch video tutorials on that one and get plenty of practice before they stopped looking like they'd been dragged through a hedge backwards.'

The mornings had been full of tears and tantrums until he'd got their hair some way close to the way Mummy did it. It had been a learning process, getting to know his daughters' physical and emotional needs following the loss of their mother, but Finn had managed this far and they'd settled into a new normal.

'I can only imagine. Can I ask what happened to their mother? If it's too personal you don't have to tell me...'

Lily wasn't the first person to ask and she wouldn't be the last but it didn't make it any easier to recount the story. He kept his back to her while he made their coffees so he didn't have to see the pity or horror in her eyes as he told the sorry tale.

'Sara was a nurse, under a lot of pressure at the hospital and working long hours. Looking back now, it was obvious she was doing too much. We never saw each other and the girls were practically living at my mum's. Unbeknown to me, she'd been having trouble sleeping and had been relying heavily on medication. I came home one night and found her in the bath. She'd taken more pills than she should have and drifted off... I'll never know if it was an accident or not.'

Although all reports had since recorded it as an accidental death, he would always have his doubts, a worry he couldn't shake that Sara's life had been so unhappy that she had decided to end it. He'd failed her as a husband and in turn failed his daughters. Since then he'd spent every day trying to make it up to them, but nothing could replace having their mother in their lives.

'I'm sure it was, Finn. She would never have intentionally left you or the girls.'

He appreciated the sentiment, but Lily

hadn't known Sara or the kind of life they'd had. No matter what anyone said, he knew he'd blame himself for the rest of his life for not being there when she'd needed him the most.

CHAPTER FOUR

LILY DID HER best to maintain her composure, even though she wanted to rush over and hug Finn to within an inch of his life. The whole nature of his wife's passing was too horrific to contemplate. From Sara's obvious distress to the idea of Finn finding her limp body in the bath, it made her want to weep for the whole family. It had clearly been devastating for them all.

She knew what it was to suffer loss, but this seemed all the more tragic given the circumstances and the two little girls left behind. Despite trying to hide his face as he'd told her of his wife's demise, the raw pain was still in evidence when he turned back to hand her a coffee. The deep grooves of worry ploughed across his forehead and the sad tilt of his mouth told of his continuing

pain. It was no surprise after everything he'd
gone through, and was still living with. All
of which she was able to relate to her own
situation.

If she had married a man like Finn, gone
on to have children, she would have caused
the same devastation when her heart condition inevitably claimed her. Further proof it
would have been selfish of her to have a family, knowing the heartache she would eventually put them through.

Finn came to join her at the breakfast bar
and they sat in silence for a few minutes sip-
ping their coffees before he ventured into
some questions of his own.

'You told the girls earlier you weren't lucky
enough to marry and have a family of your
own. Did you ever come close?'

She supposed it was natural for him to
want to know more about her when he'd
given so much of himself and his family tonight, but Lily had never really confided in
anyone about her personal problems and she
wasn't sure she was ready to do so now either.

'Not really. I guess I never met anyone

whose future gelled with mine.' That much was true. As soon as a partner mentioned the idea of marriage or children she'd known it was time to get out of the relationship because a future together was something she simply couldn't guarantee.

'You'd make a good mum. You were really good with the girls tonight.'

'Reading a bedtime story is one thing, a lifetime of responsibility is entirely different. Now, I'm sure you didn't bring me over to talk about my desolate love life. You said there were some problems you needed to discuss?' She'd already spent longer in his home than she'd intended and she was worried if she extended her visit any more she would share too much personal information. The reason she didn't was because she didn't want anyone to treat her any differently. Her heart condition didn't make her any less of a person, but not everyone would see it that way. It was easier just to deal with it alone.

She could feel Finn's eyes trying to penetrate through to the truth, but she wouldn't be drawn any further on the subject of her personal life. He stared at her a little longer before apparently giving up.

'I'm afraid I got you over here under false pretences. The project seems to be going well so far. We've had a couple of emergency medical calls, which we were able to assist with until the patients were able to be transferred to the hospital. I actually wanted to speak to you about the other day at the station.'

'Oh?' Lily was glad there were no hiccups to report, but she was confused as to why he'd felt the need to lie to her about it.

'Obviously an apology would have been better if I'd gone to you to make it, but circumstances tonight conspired against that. I…uh…wanted to say sorry about my behaviour that night. I invited you over then…'

'You couldn't wait to get rid of me when your buddies came back,' she finished for him, the memory deflating her previous good mood. Her time with the girls had made her feel wanted, needed, but that was taken away as Finn reminded her of his embarrassment at being seen with her the last time they'd been together.

'No, it wasn't like that. Well, I suppose it was, but not because of the reasons you think.' He became agitated when she challenged him, to the point he managed to knock over his coffee cup, spilling the contents over the counter and Lily. A brown waterfall of hot liquid cascaded into her lap and in her haste to back away she tipped the stool over, landing heavily on the floor.

'Ouch.' She lay dazed on the cool tiled floor, waiting for the pain at the back of her head to subside.

Finn swore before coming to help her sit up. 'Are you okay? I'm so sorry. I'm a clumsy idiot.'

Lily sat up, one hand pressing against her throbbing skull and the other trying to hold the hot, sodden fabric away from her skin.

'I'll survive, don't worry.'

'Can I get you a cold compress or a change of clothes?' He fussed around her, pulling the upturned stool away and mopping up the rest of the spilled coffee.

'I think there's a bit of a lump forming where I hit my head but it's nothing serious.'

The last couple of minutes had been a comedy of errors but without the laughs.

She heard Finn rustling in the freezer before he came back with a bag of frozen peas for her.

'This should stop the swelling,' he said, gently holding it against the injury. She flinched at first but the cool pressure was welcome. As she got to her feet, with Finn still holding the bag of peas against her head, they made eye contact and promptly both burst out laughing. It was such a ridiculous situation to have found themselves in and she'd been hurt again, all because Finn was trying to be nice to her.

'So, you wanted to apologise?' She grinned, trying to make light of the situation despite her ruined clothes and head wound.

'I'm not making a very good job of it, am I?' He offered her a lopsided smile in penance and Lily's heart did a weird flip that immediately made her take a step back, putting a little distance between them.

Despite her apprehension about coming here it had been a lovely night with the girls and she was obviously confusing that cosy scene reading them bedtime stories with something else. Just because she couldn't have a family didn't mean she didn't crave one and she was sure this growing attraction towards Finn was mixed up in that. He was part of this happy image she had of a loving dad and his children. It was a warning that she was getting too close and things would have been better if he'd remained cold towards her instead of trying so hard to be nice.

'Don't worry about it. I should probably go anyway.' She handed him back the bag of defrosting vegetables and sought to make a quick exit before she did something more humiliating than falling off a stool.

'I really am sorry, Lily. For getting you over here, for foisting the girls on you, for spilling hot coffee over you and for making you fall and bang your head. Most of all I'm sorry if I made you feel bad the other night.'

He was following behind her to the door and when she opened it he put his hand against it to stop her leaving, forcing her to turn around and face him. She didn't want to look at him, to have him see the tears welling in her eyes, or see how being reminded of his behaviour had upset her, because none of it should matter. Lily was a strong woman and had been through worse but, for reasons she didn't want to comprehend, the idea of having Finn reject her had hurt bone-deep and she hadn't been able to move past it.

Nevertheless, she sucked it all up and reacted the only way she knew how. 'Listen, Finn, I get it. No one wants to be seen with the fat girl.'

She watched him frown then dip his head as he swore. 'That's not... I don't think that...'

He made a guttural sound and hit the door with the heel of his hand. 'I wasn't embarrassed to be seen with you. I felt guilty about being with someone who wasn't my wife and enjoying the company. When the guys came in, I panicked. It was reality crashing in and making me realise you were the first woman they'd seen me with since Sara, and the shame I felt was from the betrayal of her memory. Of course the boys didn't bat an eyelid, they were simply surprised to see you there, and now I've had time to think it over I realise I overreacted.'

'Oh,' was all Lily could manage, over-whelmed both by the confession and by Finn's closeness to her. She was effectively trapped between his body and the front door, his hand still resting against the frame, caging her there. Not that she could have moved if she'd wanted, frozen by the realisation that he hadn't rejected her after all and the chemistry which she could sense brewing between them was real.

'And for the record, I think you're beautiful.' Finn brushed a stubborn tear away from the corner of her eye and the slightest touch of him against her skin almost stopped her heart. The jolt of electricity which seemed to pass between them stole her breath away.

He hadn't said he thought she was beautiful despite her size, or that she would be pretty if she lost weight, or any of the hundreds of backhanded compliments she'd heard before. Finn was telling her she was beautiful and the sincerity of those words was there in his blue eyes, looking at her as though she was the only other person in the world right now. Locked in this little bubble of longing, Lily couldn't seem to think about anything other than kissing Charlie Finnegan.

They both seemed to be resisting the pull which had drawn them so close their lips were almost touching. She could feel his warm breath on her skin, see his darkening eyes lingering on her mouth, wanting this as much as she did. Then, as if the last thread of restraint had snapped, his lips were suddenly on hers, taking and giving all at once.

Lily was swept up in his arms, the strength of his embrace matched by the ferocity of his kisses. She was lost in the dizzying sensation of passion, of being wanted, and of her own arousal. Finn was creating a need inside her she hadn't felt for a long time, an ache only he could fill, but also an awakening of something she knew to be dangerous. To give in to this lust, this want to be with him completely, was not something which could be satisfied by a one-time surrender to temptation.

She couldn't fall for Finn. He had daughters to think about, girls who had already suffered so much loss and grief to get involved with someone who couldn't be there for them in the future. It wouldn't be fair on any of them after all this time of denying herself a family, to insinuate herself into someone else's. Only to destroy them, the way the death of her father and sister had devastated her. She couldn't let that happen just because she had the hots for the man currently doing his best to kiss her into an actual swoon.

'I'm sorry, Finn. I have to go.' She broke off the kiss and fumbled for the door handle behind her back. If she didn't leave now she knew she would never find the courage to do it again, when being in his embrace felt so good.

'Tiger Lily?'

He wasn't playing fair, bestowing a pet name upon her and fixing her with those lust-dazed eyes. Especially when she was more of a mewing kitten right now than a feisty beast. Any woman would be glad to have him look at her the way he was looking at Lily. With a promise of passion and a whole lot more than fevered kisses on the doorstep. She cursed her father's legacy tonight more than ever, for stealing away her chance of happiness.

'You have your girls to think about and I'm sorry, but I never signed on for family life.'

She wasn't that lucky.

'Lily—' Finn had to take a step back as she opened the door and fled out into the night. It took him a moment to assess what had just happened and come to the conclusion that she was right and he wouldn't go chasing after her. He did have his girls to think of, along with the wife he had only recently lost. His libido and base needs paled into insignificance once he was able to think clearly again.

He closed the door on the dark night and the idea of starting a new relationship with anyone. The screech of tyres signalled Lily's similar regret over their brief lapse of judgement. Even though he'd enjoyed every second of it while it was happening. The sweet smell of her perfume tickling his senses, her soft skin beneath his fingertips and the fiery passion in her kiss were things he wouldn't easily forget. Things he had been fantasising about for some time if he was honest with himself.

They had been growing closer lately, to the point where he had missed her and made up that excuse to get her over here. His first mistake. Not only had he crossed that line between his personal and professional life, but he had introduced her to his daughters, given them reason to like her too. It would be too easy to let her slip into that void Sara had left behind, providing a much-needed female presence in all of their lives.

How wonderful it would be for them all to have someone at home again to love and care for them, to read to them, to talk to, to kiss. Except it was a fantasy he couldn't afford to invest in. Lily had said it herself, she didn't want a family and he didn't want anyone in his life who might possibly hurt his children. Having to end a relationship because he'd jumped in too early would be further damage to their emotional wellbeing and he was already burdened with the guilt of failing them.

No, they would put this lapse of sanity behind them and keep things strictly professional from now on. With things already in motion, hopefully they wouldn't even have to cross paths again. As soon as he returned the coat she'd left behind in her hurry to get away from him.

* * *

If Lily hadn't needed the lanyard with her ID on it for work she would have quite happily said goodbye to her coat for ever rather than go back to Finn's place to retrieve it. Even for the shortest spell she'd had in his house, there were too many emotive associations for her to return. Spending that time with the girls seemed to have had a profound effect on her, just as much as giving in to the attraction with Finn. Both occurrences had made her realise what she had given up to safeguard other people's hearts, when hers was aching for that companionship and loving environment she had been part of for her brief visit.

Not to mention the hot encounter she'd shared with Finn before running away from him and those feelings she'd tried so hard to avoid. Who knew all it would take was a widowed fireman to remind her she wasn't dead yet? Charlie Finnegan was as good at starting fires as he was at putting them out.

To save them both from temptation she'd texted him about retrieving her coat, arranging to meet at the station tonight, where there were plenty of other people to keep them out of harm's way.

It didn't mean her heart didn't give a joyful leap when he came down to meet her, dressed in that short-sleeved white shirt that showed off his strong thick forearms which she found inexplicably sexy.

'Hey,' she said, with all the guile of a teenage girl calling on her hot next-door neighbour.

'Hey, yourself.' All he had to do was grin to remind her of what they'd done together the last time they'd seen each other and her hormones partied as if she were eighteen again.

'I'm just here to pick up my coat,' she reiterated, hoping it would excuse the rudeness when she grabbed it and ran in the opposite direction.

He held it out at arm's length, clearly just as eager to avoid their past mistake, and discussing it, as she was.

Before she could make her escape the alarm sounded and the place was filled with bodies and noise.

'There's a fire at a house over on Main

Street. Multiple casualties. Paramedics are on their way but we'll be first on the scene,' Finn's colleague shouted over to him, warning that it was probably not going to be an easy shout.

'I should come with you.' Lily didn't have to think twice about it. These were probably people she knew, in her community, needing medical assistance. Any personal issues she had being around Finn were of no importance in the face of a potential tragedy.

'As much as we could probably use the help, you're not authorised. I'll be going in there myself tonight since we're short-staffed and I'm afraid we can't risk anyone else getting hurt.' He was already pulling on his gear, getting ready to organise his crew to face whatever was waiting out there.

'Call me later? Just let me know you're all right.'

Finn nodded and in what seemed like no time at all the engines were on their way, sirens blaring, lights flashing.

The nature of Lily's job meant she usually had some advance warning of what she was going to be dealing with, her patients having been seen and assessed by other medical staff before reaching her door. Here, they were driving into the unknown and her heart was in her mouth at the thought of what might be lying in store for him.

Lily knew this was his job and running into burning buildings was something he did every day, but being here, watching him go, brought it home to her. He could get killed. One night he could head out like this and simply never return to his family, or her. She shuddered at the thought of never seeing him again, and that was when she knew it was too late. She cared for him and there was no going back.

If she hadn't had to come back for her coat she would have found some other excuse to come and see him again. Some things were too obvious to ignore, no matter how inconvenient, and the effect Finn had on her, physically and mentally, wasn't simply going to vanish because she wished it so. Sooner or later they were going to have to address the matter, and her rapid pulse was telling her the outcome she was still hoping to have from that conversation. After all, she was the one to have walked away from the explosive chemistry, not Finn.

Hopefully he would return unscathed and they could take things from there. For now, that was all that mattered.

CHAPTER FIVE

FINN'S EVERY SENSE was engulfed by events. The smell of smoke burning the inside of his nostrils, the roar of the flames, the whoosh of water from the hoses being directed from the ground and the screams of the people inside and outside of the building were unfortunately all too familiar. The imprint of the red, yellow and orange tongues of fire flickering in the darkness would be burned onto his retinas for some time.

Once he donned his mask and breathing apparatus and forced his way inside, it seemed an eternity before he saw anything else. He was calling out for a response, some sign that there was life. All the while moving from room to room, dodging fire and flames. Eventually he moved upstairs and into what looked as though it had once been a nursery, pastel colours smudged black and grey from the devastation of the fire. Out of the corner of his eye he spotted a tiny figure in the cot and he grabbed it up and held it close to his chest. He couldn't see any movement, felt no response, but took off his own mask to cover the face of the child in the hope it would help him or her breathe.

From then on he fought like a lion to get back out of the house, battling falling debris and pushing through that fierce wall of heat to get outside again.

One of his colleagues stumbled outside shortly after him, his arms around another adult, trying to keep them upright.

'My baby!' The anguished high-pitched scream was the only indication that the person they had rescued was a woman, her entire body and clothes covered in a layer of black soot.

She lunged at the bundle in his arms he could now see was a little girl, no more than eighteen months old. Her long, once-golden locks were streaked with black dirt and grime, her eyes closed, her body still.

Despite the urge to retch, thinking of one of his own girls lying there, Finn launched into emergency mode. Falling apart was not going to help anyone now.

'There are two more upstairs,' one of the crew informed Finn as he carried the baby away from the building, shouting instructions to the rest of the men.

With no sign of the paramedics on scene, he laid the child down on a blanket and cleaned away the dirt he could see around her mouth. Thankfully the mother had been escorted away by a well-meaning member of the public so she couldn't see what was going on or hinder his progress.

With no pulse to be found, he had no choice but to begin rescue breaths, willing the little girl to fight her way back to life. His thoughts flitted to Lily and the time they'd had to do this together. Both of their jobs involved saving lives, but when they were dealing with little ones who should've had their whole lives in front of them it brought home how fragile the human body was, and sometimes not even a fireman or a cardiologist could save them.

Finn closed the child's nose using his thumb and index finger. He opened the mouth a little so it was pointing upwards before taking a breath himself and sealing his mouth around the tiny patient's. He breathed steadily, watching for the chest to begin moving, then took his mouth away again. With no response, he repeated the process a further four times.

No sign of life present meant he was forced to begin chest compressions. It was trickier to perform CPR on children and he had to be careful to ensure there was no pressure put on the ribs. With fingers interlocked he began pushing down with the heel of his hand and performed rescue breaths after every thirty chest compressions.

Eventually his prayers were answered and the little girl began to cough. As soon as Finn saw signs of life he reached for the oxygen mask kept in the back of the vehicle to aid breathing. Slowly, wonderfully, the child came round and gave a pitiful little cry. Enough for him to let out a shaky breath, relieved he had been able to prevent one tragedy. It was also sufficient to draw the mother to where Finn had been working on her daughter, tears streaking down her smoke-blackened face.

'Is she okay? Millie? Oh, Millie, thank goodness.' The mother gathered her child into her arms and he left the two of them, calling to attract the attention of the paramedics who had just arrived in the ambulance.

Unfortunately the scene there was not such a happy one. Two figures were now being wheeled by on stretchers by the ambulance crew, one completely covered from view.

Someone passed him a bottle of water, which he took a sip from before splashing the rest over his head and face, his own skin blackened from the smoke he'd battled through to reach the casualties.

'I'm afraid the father didn't make it. He apparently went back inside after raising the alarm to get the son from the upstairs bedroom.'

So much tragedy and pain in one night for a family who had probably lost everything they owned in the fire. The relief of saving the little girl was dimmed by the pain of knowing the grief they would still suffer on learning of their other loss. Finn would have done the same thing again. In fact his entire career was based on him venturing into raging infernos to save others, and one wrong move could leave his girls orphaned. It was something he was aware of every day.

This time it wasn't only the faces of his daughters which haunted him. Lily was there too, waiting for him to come home, and he didn't want to let her down. She was one more thing he had to live for.

Fire was not something exciting and thrilling to Finn but danger, a threat to life, and it had been his calling to do this job the same way Lily had been drawn to work in the medical profession. He wanted to save lives, to prevent death and grief and tragedy, probably even more so now he'd been through so much of his own. Yet he was putting his own life on the line every day to do so and there was no bigger measure of a man than his selfless need to help others. Charlie Finn was a giant among men.

Lily's stomach had been in knots, waiting

to hear from him tonight, to make sure he was safe. She had realised whilst sitting staring out of the window into the darkness of night that even if a person didn't have a death sentence hanging over them in the form of a heart condition or work in a perilous profession, life wasn't guaranteed for ever. A revelation confirmed when he had called to say he was okay but that they'd lost someone.

She'd sacrificed her personal life over the years and left herself with nothing, all for some false sense of virtue that no one except her would ever appreciate. A husband, a family and all of those events which happened along the way had been off-limits to her because of her own rules and boundaries. Now she was left wondering if she'd somehow been punishing herself for something beyond her control when she was the only one suffering as a result.

She'd seen young and old alike lose their lives over the years and never equated her life to theirs. However, sitting here tonight chewing her nails as Finn risked his life she was faced with the possibility of losing him. It wasn't something she could prevent, any more than he could predict her inevitable end. Life and death went hand in hand. They weren't things the average person could control or bend to their will. If only she had come to that conclusion years ago, before she'd become this spiky loner who couldn't let relationships stick in case they actually came to mean something.

She was still sitting in the dark, contemplating everything she'd sacrificed for apparently no good reason, when Finn arrived at her door.

'Hey,' he said, leaning into the doorframe, that lazy smile making her even more regretful about the life she had denied herself to this point.

'Hey.' She opened the door wide and walked away, letting him follow her inside. 'I wasn't expecting to see you tonight. The phone call was enough. I just wanted to know you were safe.'

'I thought I'd call in on my way home. You seemed as though you had something on your mind tonight and I thought you might need to talk to someone.'

He could add being perceptive to his list

of superhero qualities, along with his selflessness.

'You're the one who has been through a traumatic event tonight.'

'Maybe I need someone to talk to,' he said and plonked himself into one of her armchairs, frowned, got up to switch on the light and sat down again.

'Something wrong?' She knew losing someone at work stuck with you, regardless of age or circumstance, but was surprised he'd chosen to come to her.

Finn sighed. 'It's just reality hitting home that none of us are ever promised tomorrow. That, despite all my precautions or desperate need to be around for my daughters, I can't control fate.'

'Tell me about it,' Lily mumbled.

'No, you tell me about it, Tiger Lily. There's clearly something bugging you.'

'Why do you keep calling me that?'

He gave her a cheeky grin in response. 'When you're riled your claws come out, Tiger Lily.'

'I'm a vicious cat?'

'No, you're defensive, lashing out when

anyone gets too close, but I'm prepared to brave the scratches to get to know you better. I owe you for helping get my kids to bed, and I can tell there's something going on with you other than forgetting to pay your electric bill.' He was trying to make a joke about the weird sight he'd found on arrival, the house in darkness with her sitting here like some dormant spirit just waiting for someone to haunt.

She took a deep breath and prepared to share the secret which had ruled her adult life, then perhaps she would be able to move on into her afterlife.

'I never had children because I have a genetic heart condition, dilated cardiomyopathy. I lost my father and sister to the disease and it devastated me. Iris was only ten and I guess my dad was still young at forty-two when he died. I decided it was better for me to be on my own than to ever put anyone through the grief my mum and I suffered. I didn't want to bring more lives into the world, only to hand them a death sentence either. So I've concentrated on my career and any relationships have been short-lived.'

Finn had been listening intently, his forehead furrowed into a frown. 'Surely loving you means accepting whatever the future holds together?'

It sounded so simple when he said it, but she had never been with anyone she thought she couldn't live without or who was prepared to take on her medical problems when she explained her circumstances to them. She was fine for a fling but long-term she was not a safe bet.

'Perhaps I've never been loved,' she joked, though the truth in those words struck deep. It wasn't something that she'd let bother her before now, telling herself that was the way she wanted it. Love made things complicated and painful and she'd done her best to avoid that. The result being that she now had no one in her life to turn to for the comfort and support Finn was giving her now out of pity.

'I doubt that.'

She ignored his attempt to soft soap her. It wasn't necessary. She knew the woman she'd been, and she'd purposely made it hard for anyone to love her. Including herself at times.

'Anyway, sitting here tonight, waiting for news on whether you were alive or dead, made me think and you're spot on, we're not guaranteed anything in life except death. I've realised that tonight, perhaps too late. I've sacrificed having a normal life for…for nothing.' She threw up her hands, the futility of it all suddenly overwhelming her, her eyes filling with liquid regret for the woman she could've been.

Finn reached across the gap between them to take her hand and reconnect. 'I'm so sorry, Lily. You can still live your life to the fullest. Better late than never, eh?'

He tried to make a joke because he didn't know what else to say or how to process the bombshell she'd just dropped. Outwardly she appeared to be a self-contained, confident professional woman. No one would have guessed that inside she was so troubled and fragile. It showed a lot of trust in him that she was opening up to him like this. Even if it was sounding more alarm bells for him.

His reasons for coming over tonight hadn't been entirely selfless. He had known there was something on her mind but he'd also wanted to see her again.

It had been a long night. He was used to that, but every loss was one too many and he always felt it, down to his very soul. More so since losing Sara. Another widowed partner, more children left without a parent and enough tears shed to put the fire out which started it all in the first place—a scenario he wouldn't wish on anyone.

It was all part of his chosen career, but it was something he would never get used to. As in all emergency services, death was something they were supposed to compartmentalise to let them continue to function in their job, but a person would have to be inhuman not to carry some residual trauma after an event like tonight. Lily had been the one person he'd wanted to see to give him some comfort. She understood the job, and him, better than people he had known for a lot longer.

'Do you ever have any regrets?' Either she didn't hear his comment or she chose to ignore it, changing the subject completely.

'Who doesn't?' he said with a yawn, the events of tonight catching up with him too. It would only be a few hours before the girls would be up, looking for their breakfast, and he wanted to be there this morning more than ever.

'If you'd known your wife would die when your girls were so young, do you think you would have still had a family?' She turned to look at him now, but the shock of hearing her question must have registered on his face as she added, 'Sorry. That was insensitive of me.'

Finn didn't know what had prompted that. Perhaps it was the untimely death they had witnessed tonight, or another reminder of the family she'd never had, but it was clear Lily was the one with regrets. However, the mere mention of his wife and everything she had left behind plunged that dagger of pain straight back into his heart. It was a loss he would never be able to explain or get over.

He strengthened himself against the tidal wave of memories flooding back. Their wedding day, the birth of the girls. Then the devastating memory of finding her in the bath, lifeless in his arms as he cried for everything they had lost.

'I can't imagine ever being without my

girls, and we had some good times. So I guess the answer's yes, I would still have had our girls even if we'd known our time together was going to be short. It's better to have lived our life together for as long as we had than never to have experienced the joy of having our family.' It might not be the answer she'd wanted but it was the truth. He had the good memories of their time together, which he hoped some day would overshadow the bad ones. As for the girls, they were his everything, the reason he got up in the morning and their happiness more important to him than his own.

Lily promptly burst into wretched, messy tears. This unravelling was such a contrast to the composed adversary he'd first encountered at that mediation meeting, he couldn't help but rush to her side, desperate to provide her with some comfort. He needed to do something for her which didn't involve pulling her into his embrace and kissing her tears away.

Although he was honoured that she had shared a very personal issue with him, it had reminded him of why he shouldn't be here offering her a shoulder to cry on. If that was all he was doing there wouldn't be a problem, but this constant craving to be with her, this longing he felt when he was with her, couldn't go anywhere. Now, more than ever, he had reason to fight this growing attraction to his Tiger Lily. She'd given him all the ammunition he could ever need to avoid getting entangled with her.

He didn't know a whole lot about her condition but it had been enough to take her sibling, a parent, and rule her life this far. Enough to disrupt the lives of him and his daughters. It might seem insensitive, and he felt for Lily and everything she had gone through, but he had to protect his girls from any further pain. He could be a friend to Lily, a colleague, but anything more than that, knowing her circumstances, would mean inviting heartache into all of their lives. Judging by her past relationships, she didn't need that any more than he did.

Yet he still wanted to do something to comfort her instead of ignoring her pain. The last time he'd done that he'd lost Sara and he wouldn't—couldn't—go through that again. He wouldn't fail another woman he cared for.

'Why don't I run you a bath and make you a cup of tea? That's my mother's cure-all.'

Lily looked at him as though he'd suggested getting in with her. As much as he would like to, he was thinking more along the lines of making her comfortable so he could go home and avoid any further temptation.

'Why would you do that? You're the one who was working and went through a very traumatic experience by the sound of it.'

'I had a quick wash and change before I came over. Is it too much to let me do one nice thing for you, Lily?'

'Does that include the tea-making?' she asked, already looking a little brighter.

'Of course.' Finn headed straight for the bathroom and set to work, adding a selection of fancy oils and potions to the big bath tub. It was the perfect way to help her relax, along with a cup of tea or a huge bar of chocolate. Whichever brought those much-needed feel-good endorphins he usually got simply from being with his daughters after a tough shift.

He filled the bath until the foamy bubbles

were in danger of spilling out onto the bath-room floor and went in search of Lily.

'All ready when you are, madam.'

'Thanks, Finn.' He could just about make out her smile, but all he could hear was sad-ness. There was a rustle as she unfurled her-self from the foetal position she'd been in on the sofa and got to her feet.

He handed her the towel he'd extracted from the bathroom closet and made sure not to touch her again. The last time he'd got too close and crossed that line between want-ing and having he'd sent her running. Lily needed support and that was all he should be offering.

Thankfully she took the towel and headed towards the bathroom without another word or look which would make him think twice about letting her bathe alone. Once he ful-filled his promise of making her a strong cup of tea his job would be done and he could go home with a clear conscience where Lily Riordan was concerned.

CHAPTER SIX

ALL LILY WANTED to do was crawl under the bedcovers and never come out again.

Liar.

What she really wanted was for Finn to carry her there and give her such a good time she would never have to think about everything she had missed out on over the years.

Instead, she stripped off and sank into the warm bath he had kindly drawn for her. The bubbles crackled in her ears as she lowered herself under the water and tried to wash away the realisation she'd thrown her life away.

Lily thought about her own grief when she'd lost her father and sister, and of Finn's words. He would rather have lived with the pain of his loss and had the happy times than never have started his family at all. The same was probably true of the victims' loved ones tonight. It all went to show she had been living a lie this whole time. She hadn't been trying to protect anyone but herself by not getting close to anyone. Now she was all alone and when her time finally came she wouldn't even have those good memories of family or relationships to cling on to.

Full of self-pity, and mourning the life she might have had, she couldn't stop the tears from falling. She sat up, clutching her knees to her body, the closest she could get to a hug when she had pushed away everyone who had ever got close. Including Finn. Only the other night she might have let herself experience one evening of pleasure, of belonging, but the moment she'd thought it could lead to something she'd run out. He was only here now out of pity, knowing she didn't have anyone to go home to the way he did.

She sobbed as though decades of self-denial, loneliness and regret had finally bubbled to the surface, and she worried she might never stop. It was too late for her to find love, to be loved the way she longed for, and it was her own fault.

* * *

Finn added sugar to the tea, hoping it would help with whatever else was ailing Lily tonight. It wasn't going to solve her problems but he hoped the gesture would make her realise she didn't have to go through whatever this was alone. Perhaps if he'd done the same for Sara, been there to run her bath and bring her a cup of tea when she'd needed it, things might have been different.

He intended to leave the tea outside the bathroom door and was ready to knock when he heard noises from inside. Listening to the gut-wrenching sound of Lily crying, great heaving sobs which seemed to come from her very soul. Whatever she was going through, it was obviously raw and painful and something she shouldn't be dealing with alone.

'Lily? Are you all right in there?' He knocked gently on the door and waited for a response.

The crying stopped but she didn't reply. He tried knocking again but the ensuing silence brought back those dark memories of his wife's last moments. That deathly quiet, the horror which had met him on the other side of the door and desperately trying to get her body out of the water. He didn't want to ever feel that powerless again.

'Lily, if you don't answer I'm coming in, so you might want to cover yourself up.' He braced himself with a deep breath, holding that oxygen in his lungs until he was sure she was all right and he was able to release it.

The sight he found, whilst still upsetting, was a relief. Lily was hugging her knees, rocking in the bath, silently crying her heart out. He set the cup of tea down and went to her, kneeling at the side of the bath. It was clear she didn't want to talk, but he wanted to show her she had someone who cared about her and who would be there when she was upset.

Since she hadn't screamed at him to get out, Finn took it as a sign she was comfortable with him being here. He took a sponge from the edge of the bath and dipped it into the bathwater, gently wiping away the tears coursing over her smooth skin. He squeezed the sponge and let the warm water cascade over her back. Lily closed her eyes and let him bathe her, a privilege from someone who was usually so guarded around him.

He lathered some shampoo into her hair before rinsing it off again with clean water. When he was sure he'd done all he could for her and he saw her fingertips begin to prune, he held up a large towel for her. He turned away to protect her modesty as she stepped out, then he wrapped her up like a burrito and swept her easily into his arms. She didn't protest but wrapped her arms around his neck and snuggled into his chest. He wondered when was the last time anyone had shown her a little love, when she seemed so in need of it.

'Where's your bedroom?'

She lifted a hand to point, but even that seemed to require too much energy. It was as if the events of the night, and whatever emotional turmoil was going on inside Lily's head, had completely physically drained her. In all their previous encounters she had given him the impression she would rather die than accept help, yet here he was, bathing and carrying her to bed like a helpless child.

He set her down on top of the mattress, still clad in her towel. If they had been a couple he wouldn't have thought twice about helping her get ready for bed and putting her under the covers, but he thought he had probably seen more of Lily than she would usually be comfortable with as it was.

'If you need anything at all, just call or text me. You have my number.' He didn't like leaving her like this, looking so lost curled up on the bed, her wet hair clinging around her face, make-up washed away to make her appear younger and more vulnerable than ever.

'Stay with me. At least for a little while.' The plea reached deep inside to play a lament on his heartstrings, making it impossible for him to walk away now. There was no way he could leave her here like this. He'd never forgive himself if anything happened to her too. What harm could it do to offer her some company and emotional support? They both knew nothing could happen between them, no matter the temptation of being in the same bed.

'I'll have to be back before the girls get up,' he said, climbing onto the mattress beside her. As she tucked her head in under his arm, he kicked off his shoes and closed his eyes. All he was doing was providing a little comfort. Once she was asleep he'd let himself out and check in with her again later. In the meantime, he'd rest his eyes too. It had been a long, tiring night for both of them.

At first Lily wondered where she had woken up, a large wall surrounding her and preventing her from getting out. Then it moved and she heard a little snore, reminding her she was in bed—with Finn. She lifted her head to glance at him. He looked at home in her bed, filling the side of the mattress which usually served to remind her she was alone. Thanks to Finn, during one of the lowest points of her life, she hadn't been.

Whatever did or didn't happen between them from now on, she would always remember the kindness he had shown bathing her, lying here with her, and showing her a compassion she had never known before. He had been so tender and understanding, letting her cry it out while supporting and taking care of her.

She didn't know how to explain what she'd gone through last night to herself, never mind

Finn, but if it had shown her anything it was that every second in life counted and she had wasted so many. All this time on her own, pushing loved ones away in an effort to avoid hurting anyone long-term, had been a kind of self-flagellation. A punishment she had bestowed upon herself because she believed her medical condition made her unworthy of the life everyone else took for granted. The tears last night had been a kind of mourning for everything she'd denied herself—a partner, children, love.

She was hoping this wake-up call hadn't come too late. The man beside her was amazing, in public and in private. If she hadn't been so stubborn they might have had something. *No*, she reminded herself, *too much baggage*. It was one thing deciding she might have got it wrong where relationships were concerned, quite another to take on a widower with two small children. She might have had a revelation but she still had to consider the feelings of others. Her fate hadn't changed simply because her mindset about it had.

'Morning.' Finn's voice was husky from sleep as he caught her watching him.

'Hey.' She had that momentary feeling of embarrassment from recounting earlier events which usually came after a night of raucous partying. Unfortunately, she did not have the excuse of alcohol or high spirits to explain away what had happened.

'How are you feeling?' He rolled over onto his side, propping his head up on one elbow, and her heart gave a little flutter. He was gorgeous as well as kind and compassionate. The complete package. For someone who could allow herself to take on a ready-made family.

'Better. Thank you.' If he hadn't come to her door last night, Lily would probably still be sitting in the dark, crying and feeling sorry for herself. She'd had her moment and he'd been right there with her until it had passed. It wasn't lost on her how generous that had been of him, sacrificing that time with his daughters to comfort her. A sign that he might have some feelings towards her too, even if there were many reasons why he wouldn't act on them either.

'Good. I was worried about you.'

'Sorry for keeping you away from your family.'

'Don't be silly. It was more important for me to know you were okay. Besides, the girls will still be asleep.'

Lily wasn't used to having anyone put her first, including herself. It was nice. Especially when she knew how devoted he was to his children. When she thought about the circumstances and how worried he'd been about her she could have slapped herself. He'd told her about his wife and how he'd found her lifeless in the bath. Lily's pity party must have brought back traumatic memories for him. It was no wonder he'd been afraid to leave her on her own, probably convinced history would repeat itself.

'I shouldn't have made you worry. It was incredibly selfish of me.'

'You were upset. You don't have to apologise, Lily. I'm simply glad you're okay.'

'It just seemed to hit me last night about how much of my life I've wasted. You said you would rather have had that short time with your wife than never being with her and it touched a nerve. That love you had for her, the strength of love that man had for his son to go back into that fire... I'll never have that and it's my own fault.' She didn't want to get morose about it again but every time she thought about the people she had pushed away, the opportunities she might have had, it was impossible not to have that ache in her chest for the life she could have had.

'It's not too late, you know.' He was trying to be optimistic on her behalf that she might still meet someone and fall in love, but it seemed too little too late. What was the point of getting into something now, when she was past her best and heading for middle age?

'I'm over forty, fat and set in my ways. It doesn't make me a catch.' She could just imagine sticking her profile pic on one of those dating apps and getting tumbleweeds in response.

'Stop saying that. I don't like it when you talk about yourself like that. You're beautiful.'

She cringed at his words. 'You don't have to say things like that to make me feel better. I know what I am, Finn.'

He huffed out a breath, but she wasn't trying to frustrate him. Lily was simply saying what she believed was the truth. She'd spent her youth building her career, batting away potential love interests, and now the bloom had well and truly faded she couldn't expect to be snapped up simply because she'd decided she didn't want to be alone any more.

What was worse, Finn was the first man who'd ever made her regret her life choices and she'd blown any chance she had with him by telling him about the ticking time bomb that was her heart.

'Why do you think you're not worthy of love, Lily? Who put that into your head?' It was the second time she had brought up the subject of her weight and he couldn't understand the reason behind the issue. People came in all shapes and sizes and it wasn't a reflection of who they were on the inside. Not that he had a problem with the way Lily looked. Other than the fact he was attracted to her and couldn't seem to bring himself to leave her bed. Lily was usually so confident in everything she did he couldn't help but think this insecurity about her appearance had been a seed planted by someone else and it had grown like an unruly, intrusive weed. He'd certainly never given her cause to think she was anything other than beautiful when he had difficulty keeping his hands off her most of the time.

'Oh, just an ex.' She tried to dismiss it as a non-event but Finn wasn't so easily fooled when the painful memory was blazing so clearly in her eyes.

'Uh-huh. So you were with some waste of space who didn't appreciate you for who you are and you've lived every day since looking at yourself through his eyes? Why would you even give him thinking room in your head?' Finn's body tensed when talking about someone he'd never met but was prepared to take to task for everything he'd done to hurt this woman.

'I guess Pearce is tied in to that whole time of getting my diagnosis and how it made me feel about myself. I did pack on a few pounds because of the condition but in hindsight the weight thing was probably an excuse so he didn't have to support me through my illness.' She snorted.

'He was fun for going out to bars and dinner parties with but he would never have made a good partner long-term. Probably why I got together with him in the first place. I didn't want someone for any more than that. At least until I had my condition confirmed, then I could've done with someone to support me rather than make me feel worse about myself.'

'He sounds like a real swell guy,' Finn emitted through gritted teeth. It was no wonder she had a complex if she'd been getting criticism at home during such a challenging time. That, wrapped up with her diagnosis, explained why she'd projected her insecurities onto him after that first dinner, and why she'd assumed the worst of him.

'Listen, that Pearce doesn't know what he's talking about. You are gorgeous, *my* Tiger Lily, and I wouldn't be here or saying these things if you weren't special.' He had to be honest with her and himself about the feelings he had for her. They both deserved that much at least after the loss and heartache they'd gone through, now they were finding solace in one another.

Lily's circumstances might have been different but he was sure she wasn't any less lonely than he had been since losing his wife. At least he had the girls, even if he sometimes felt as though he was acting the part as a parent, putting on that brave façade in order to hold things together when he was falling apart inside. Lily had no one and seemed to think that was her fate because of something beyond her control. She didn't see herself the way he saw her—fierce, kind, an amazing doctor and a beautiful person. There were a million reasons why they shouldn't be together, why he shouldn't be tempting fate by lying in her bed, but that didn't stop the wanting, or the need to show her she was worthy of loving.

'Really?' Lily looked up at him with such disbelief it was Finn's undoing.

If she wasn't going to listen to what he was telling her, he'd have to show her. He tilted his head and kissed her softly on the lips. A taste which only made him want more. She was fiery and sweet, tender and passionate, all in one kiss. Everything he could want.

Lily pressed her body closer to his so

he could feel her warmth even through his clothes. He wanted more, but that came with risks he wasn't sure either of them should really be taking.

'Do you believe me now?' he asked, his voice, his body, his mind, all pulsing with desire for this woman lying next to him, who didn't realise how beautiful she was, inside and out.

She opened her eyes and he all but drowned in her sapphire gaze. 'Hmm, I might need a little more persuading.'

That uncertainty seemed to have disappeared during the course of the kiss, replaced with the confident Lily he knew better. A greater turn-on, if it had been needed. She wanted this as much as he did.

He kissed her again, this one building into something more passionate and urgent with every passing moment. Their lips clashing together, tongues searching for one another, hands grabbing each other, so they could be as close as possible.

'Is this okay?' He broke off the kiss to get her consent before they went any further, knowing she was vulnerable and not wanting to take advantage of that in any shape or form. If he thought for one second she wasn't sure he would put a halt to proceedings, no matter how painful for him.

'Yes. Make love to me, Finn.' Lily instigated the kissing this time, and began tugging his T-shirt up his chest. All the confirmation he could have wished for to make the next move.

Goodness knew he wanted to, but lust could only blind him to the reasons he shouldn't for so long. He let out a groan of frustration.

'We shouldn't be doing this.'

'Why not? Don't we deserve to have some happiness, Finn?' She reached up to cup his face in her hands and he knew she needed this as much as he did. He also knew she had as many reasons not to get involved with him too.

'I'm not denying that, but a relationship is a complication neither of us need right now. We're both going through…a lot. I appreciate you being honest with me about your problems and honestly, to the right person that won't matter, but I have the girls to think about. I can't bring someone into their lives, it will only confuse them.' He rolled away from temptation, trying to compose himself and think clearly without lust clouding his judgement.

Lily shifted onto her side to look at him. 'We don't have to rush into anything. This is just between us. I'm not asking for anything serious, Finn. I don't need the complications. But I do want you.'

She grabbed the front of his shirt and pulled him down, kissing him full and firm on the lips, marking her territory and her desire all at the same time. His head was buzzing with the implications and the pleasures of taking this further.

He wanted Lily too, but they both knew her medical issues were something he would have to be wary of if she became part of the girls' lives when they'd already suffered so much loss. She was making this easier by taking the idea of a serious commitment out of the equation, but was that the kind of man he was? The truth was he didn't know. He'd never had a one-night, or a one-morning, stand with anyone. Never even *been* with anyone other than Sara.

'I'm not denying the feeling's mutual, but I don't want things to get messy. I can't promise you anything, Lily, and we still have to work together.' He didn't want to trick her into believing there could be more to this than sex and risk hurting her when it became apparent he wasn't offering her anything more than that.

'Hey, I'm not asking for a wedding ring. It could be a one-time thing.'

'To get it out of our systems, you mean? Does that ever work?'

'It works for me.' Then Lily's hands were tugging at his shirt, urging him to get naked. She wanted to live in the moment instead of worrying about the future, encouraging him to do the same. He couldn't tell her not to live her life based on what-ifs, then do the same thing himself.

He liked Lily, he was sure she liked him back and that should be enough for now. Sara was gone but he still had many years ahead of him and he didn't want to be alone for ever because of loyalty to his deceased wife. Lily was the first woman who had made him rethink the idea of facing the rest of his life alone and, even though they were staying away from the idea of commitment, he had been without joy for long enough. Something he knew he could find with Lily, for however long they had together. He couldn't keep his life on hold for ever. Every now and then he had to act on impulse, on his feelings, and right now they were telling him to get naked.

He stripped off his shirt and Lily leaned into him, kissing her way across his collarbone, her feather-light touch driving him wild, so barely there it made him question if he'd felt it all.

She grew bolder the more she explored his chest with her mouth and, when she reached his nipple, washing her tongue over the sensitive skin until all of him was standing to attention.

'Lily, it's been a while for me. I don't want to peak too soon. Besides, I'm supposed to be the one making love to you.' He rolled her over onto her back with a primitive groan. There was nothing he wanted more than to fill her, to experience that ultimate joy of forging their bodies together as lust consumed them, but they both needed more. He wanted this to last, to enjoy one another for as long as they could. Once reality dawned there was no way of knowing what would happen between them.

He kissed the skin behind her ear, revelling in the little gasp it elicited. She was so responsive to his touch it made him want to investigate further, find all of her sensitive spots and pleasure her until she was spent.

Slowly, he untucked the towel and unwrapped Lily's voluptuous body so she was lying there like a delicious candy, making his mouth water.

As she bit her lip and her breathing became rapid, he could see she was nervous about being so exposed to him, so he took off the rest of his clothes, leaving them both naked, with nowhere to hide. Not that he would want her to. Despite her self-deprecating comments about her figure, Lily was everything he had fantasised about. Those feminine curves and full breasts had been the reason he'd questioned his ability to remain celibate for the rest of his life. He was a red-blooded male with a fire burning inside him to have her every time he saw her and he couldn't believe he was lucky enough to bring that fantasy to life.

'You're making me anxious, staring at me like that. Come here.' She tried to pull him back down, to cover her body with his, but Finn hadn't finished his perusal of her sexy figure.

He shook his head, grinning as he lowered his head and began to kiss his way across her skin. This time he was determined to get the upper hand where Lily was concerned, leaving her at the mercy of his attentions, and hopefully her own orgasm.

Taking the weight of one breast in his hand, he teased her nipple until it was straining for the attention of his mouth. Dutifully, he sucked the tight pink bud, leaving Lily moaning a plea for more. As he licked his way around the dusky areola, he pinched her other nipple between his fingers and she bucked beneath him, writhing in ecstasy.

He was loath to leave the sensitive nubs of her full breasts but there were so many other places he wanted to explore he didn't want to miss anything. Trailing the tip of his tongue down her torso, he moved further down the bed, and down Lily's spreadeagled body, until he came to that little patch of curly hair nestled between her thighs. She sucked in a sharp breath and, before she could exhale, Finn plunged his tongue into her wetness. After her initial shock, her limbs went limp and she seemed to surrender to everything he was doing to her. A clear sign she was enjoying it as much as he was.

He gripped her soft thighs to give him purchase as he drove deep inside, tasting and teasing until they were both panting for more. That desire to make her come hastened his pace, his tongue licking and swirling as he sought her orgasm like a man possessed. Giving her no time to think or come down from the high of her obvious arousal, he sucked on that most intimate part and found her breaking point. Lily cried out as her climax coated them both and Finn could wait no longer to claim his satisfaction too.

He slid his throbbing erection into her slick heat and gave a muffled groan with his face buried in the crook of her neck. It took him a moment to regain his composure and resist the urge to give in to his pleasure too soon when it was something to be savoured. Lily felt so good he wanted to stay there for ever.

'Are you okay?' He was aware that it had been a while for her too and he didn't want to do anything she wasn't ready for, regardless that her body was responding so readily to his every touch.

'I'm good.' She chuckled, that jiggle of her body against his stimulating him further.

With Lily's permission he was free to continue his pursuit, striving to reach that pinnacle of ecstasy himself. Lily was a willing participant on the journey, her every kiss on the lips, and squeeze of her inner muscles around his rock-hard shaft, urging him closer to release. He pushed inside her again and again without restraint, his breathing and pace becoming frantic. Lily's eyes were locked onto his, the intensity of what was happening between their bodies reflected in her dark pupils. He watched as she bit her lip, as her forehead furrowed and her mouth fell open, a cry of ecstasy piercing the dark room, and he could hold back no longer. The wet rush of her orgasm as she tightened around him ripped a roar of elation from his chest and he poured inside her.

In that moment nothing else mattered except how she'd made him feel. Complete. Given the chance he would happily spend every second of every day here, their bodies entwined and fitting perfectly together. He was content, he was happy, and he was a very lucky man.

CHAPTER SEVEN

LILY HAD BEEN rendered speechless. Not only was she out of breath from their physical exertions but she was lost for words after what they'd just shared. Neither of them had apparently seen it coming, yet she was sure they'd both been fighting it for their own reasons. Now Finn was lying here, looking at her with a silly grin on his face as if he wanted to do it all again.

Usually—though it had been a while since she'd shared a bed with anyone else—during this post-coital awkward stage, she tried to cover up. Once the passion of the moment had passed she became aware of her lumps and bumps on display. Finn's hungry gaze emboldened her so she was quite happy to lie naked on top of the covers. He was a boost for her self-esteem and seemed to accept her not only for how she looked on the outside, but also the challenges she was facing in the future.

Of course sleeping together was no promise of anything beyond getting their breath back, but for now it gave her hope all wasn't lost. He had shown her she could still be wanted and didn't have to be alone for however long she had left on the earth. Being with Finn had helped her move from despair into ecstasy and it would be heaven if she could have this on a regular basis, though she was aware he had responsibilities she wasn't a part of, and had no desire to be.

'As much as I would like to lie here with you, I'm going to have to get home for the girls.' Finn vocalised what she knew was coming, but still didn't want to happen. It meant she would end up alone again.

'I know, I've taken up too much of your time.'

He scowled at her. 'I am definitely not complaining. Believe me, I'm sorry I have to leave.'

The little bird of hope which had been flapping its wings in her chest since the moment he'd kissed her took flight, soaring dangerously close to the sun. Despite her current euphoria, she had to be careful not to get too carried away or she might get burned. She'd been protecting herself for so long. Now that she had opened herself up to the idea of romance and relationships, a rejection could scar her for ever. Although they had given in to the attraction on the basis that this was a one-off, Finn had given her the confidence to at least believe there was a chance for more, and a reason to query the possibility.

'Do you think we could do this again some time?'

Finn smiled and dropped a lingering kiss on her lips. 'I would like to but, as I said before, I'm not ready to get into a relationship.'

'We don't have to be anything serious. We can keep it casual. I don't think either of us is ready for anything more than that. I mean, I'm not going to beg, but the offer is there. We're both adults, with needs. This could be good for us.'

She wanted the best of both worlds—great sex without having to make any serious commitment. That was a step she wasn't ready to take, and certainly not with someone who had two young impressionable girls. She'd seen how excited they'd been when she'd turned up on the doorstep. Not only did she want to avoid upsetting them, but she was keen to dodge an insta-family situation. After spending most of her adult life keeping people at arm's length it would be a shock to her system to suddenly find herself playing stepmother to someone else's children. For now it would be enough to simply continue seeing Finn in private.

'Tempting, very tempting…' he muttered against her neck, kissing and nibbling at her skin, and she wasn't sure he was even listening to her.

'Finn… I thought you had to go.' Lily saw no point in getting her worked up if he was going to leave her here, alone and frustrated.

'I'm sure we can manage another thirty minutes. Who needs sleep anyway?' With a growl he captured her mouth with his and she could feel his hard member already pressing against her thigh.

'A whole half hour together? Then why are we wasting a single second?' If this did turn out to be their one and only bedroom tryst, she wanted him to remember it and think of her as more than the doctor who'd had a breakdown in her bath.

This time she straddled him, determined to make the most of their time together. She ground her hips against him, the lower half of her body grazing along his. Finn cupped her breasts, kneading the soft flesh and playing with her nipples until she was wet and ready for him.

Taking him in hand, she teased the tip of his erection along her inner thighs before sinking down along his shaft. He filled her completely, making her gasp with the satisfaction of feeling him inside her. Her body instinctively took over, rocking slowly against him at first and gradually picking up speed. She braced her hands on his chest as she rode him and it wasn't long before his hands were on her hips as he thrust up to meet her in response.

The pressure of her impending climax was already building and she was powerless to resist it, having experienced it once already and knowing that utter bliss of finally giving in to it. Everything Finn did to her body reminded her she was very much alive and though it had let her down in some areas, sex could still be an important part of her life. Although she was sure she would only ever want it with Finn.

He sat up then, took one of her nipples in his mouth and tugged it between his teeth, sending a tidal wave of arousal shooting through her and leaving her at his mercy.

Finn took advantage of the distraction and switched places so she was the one now lying flat on her back. He kissed her fully on the lips as he pushed inside her, giving her exactly what she needed. They climbed the peak together, bodies in synch, hot breath mingling, eyes locked onto one another. When she reached her orgasm Finn followed close behind. It was as though they knew exactly what the other needed, perfectly in tune, even their chests rising and falling in harmony.

'I'm done with you now. You can go,' she joked, knowing they couldn't delay his return home any longer. It wouldn't be fair on him or the girls.

'Glad to have been of service.' He jumped

out of bed and collected his clothes from the floor before disappearing off to the bathroom.

Lily watched his naked backside as he walked away and gave a contented sigh. She'd had no idea when she'd come up with the idea of the fire brigade working with the hospital that they would end up here. Perhaps if she had the project would have gone ahead without her because this feeling she had was something she'd been trying to avoid for a long time.

She was falling in love with Finn and she knew it would only end in tears. Most likely hers.

'I don't want my hair in a ponytail, Daddy. I want to have it down, like Lily.'

'Fine.' Finn gave up trying to style the hair of a fidgety five-year-old and simply put a clip in the front to keep it from falling in Niamh's eyes.

'I've been hearing a lot about this Lily,' his mother piped up from the corner of the room. It was a rare Saturday morning off for him and they had planned to go out for the day.

He should have been prepared for the inquisition, especially when he'd been so late coming from Lily's a couple of days ago.

They'd both been busy with work since, but had kept in touch with a few sexy text messages. There was no denying he'd enjoyed their night together, but this was new territory for him. He didn't have any regrets about sleeping with Lily, but he did have to pause and think about what they were doing and how it might affect his children. Some time apart from her would clear his head so he wasn't constantly thinking about how much he wanted to do it all over again.

'She's the cardiologist I'm working with on this new scheme. I'm sure you saw her on the TV with me.'

'Oh, that's her? She's very pretty. And unmarried, I hear.' His mother helped Maeve into her coat and pretended that she was simply making casual conversation rather than fishing for information on her son's personal life.

She had been very vocal of late about how he should be getting back out there to meet someone so he didn't spend the rest of his life alone. Something he'd had no interest in until he'd met Lily. His mother would be over the moon to know he had found a woman he liked, more than liked if it wasn't too scary to admit to himself. However, that was the problem. Finn didn't want his mum, or anyone else, to get carried away by the fact he'd met someone when he couldn't predict what, if anything, it would lead to.

'She's also a very busy doctor.' He wasn't about to give his mother reason to think she should be buying a hat for their wedding. She meant well, but Finn didn't need the added pressure of his mum interfering in his love life.

It was still strange to even think he had one after the death of his wife, and something he needed to get used to. At least by keeping things casual he could back away if it turned out he wasn't ready even for that.

'Uh-huh. Well, the girls like her…'

'Lily read us bedtime stories,' Niamh added in support of the idea that she would make a suitable match. It would definitely have made a difference if the children hadn't taken to her, but they were clearly fans already. That would put him under more pressure to make things work if their budding relationship should ever be made public.

'She's a very likeable person. Now, are we ready to go?' He opened the front door to chivvy everyone out, and hopefully put an end to the conversation.

'Okay, okay, I'll drop the subject—'

'Good.'

'Suffice to say, you're still a relatively young and handsome man and this Lily seems like a nice, child-friendly woman. I know you loved Sara, but she would want you to be happy. When your father died I swore I'd never want to be with anyone else, but it has been lonely, Charlie, and maybe if I'd been able to open my heart again I would have had a different life.' His mother shrugged her shoulders and for the first time Finn noticed a sadness in her usually twinkling blue eyes.

He was so used to having her support, a babysitter and agony aunt on hand, he'd never really wondered if it was a fulfilling enough life. Children by their very nature were selfish, only thinking about their wants and needs, neglecting those of their parents, and he included himself in that group. Since his father's death when he'd been very young, she'd spent her days looking after him, and now her granddaughters too. Finn had taken it for granted, but now he was made to question if that life would be enough for him in the future.

It was going to be a balancing act between his love life and family life and he needed to get things right when he'd messed up so much with Sara.

'I'm sorry if I've never said this, Mum, but I appreciate everything you've done for me and the kids. I don't know how I would've got through this past year without you, but we're good now. If you ever need time out or there's something on that you want to go to, please just say. I don't want to stop you living your life.'

He grabbed his mum into a bear hug, which quickly became a pile-on as the girls flung their arms around them too. They didn't even know what they were hugging for, but they were such loving little girls they didn't need an excuse for cuddles. Their sensitive, car-ing nature was even more reason that Finn didn't intend to drag them into his relationship with Lily. He didn't want them to get too attached, the way he already was.

Lily checked her phone again, but there hadn't been any messages from Finn today. Usually she didn't have any problem resting when she had some down time but she was restless and not hearing from him had put her on edge too. Every ping notifying her of a message had put a smile on her face, knowing it was another saucy comment from her sexy fireman, but now she was worried he was cooling off.

In the heat of the moment they hadn't been able to get enough of each other, but perhaps now he was back in family life and they'd had time apart he'd realised even a fling wasn't feasible. At least she'd been upfront with him about her heart condition, even if it had put him off the idea of anything more serious between them.

It wouldn't have been the first time, but she'd thought Finn was different. He'd told her accepting her should mean accepting that

part of her which had ruined every other relationship, but only time would tell if he was
ready to make any sort of commitment to that
uncertain future before her. Or if she even
wanted that.

For now she would go to her happy place
and dressed accordingly. Wearing her puffy
waterproof coat, wellies and her scarf
wrapped well around her neck, she set off
out of her door for the seashore.

Lily closed her eyes and listened to the
gentle lapping sound as the tide washed out
over the sand and soothed her soul. She didn't
need anyone or anything when she was out
here. Although she would be lying if she said
she wasn't still waiting to hear that sharp
ping connecting her with Finn.

So much so, she thought she'd imagined
him calling her name.

'Lily?'

She opened her eyes seconds before she
was body-slammed by two tiny figures.

'Lily!'

'Hey, you two…three.' She spotted Finn
walking towards her too. So she hadn't imagined him after all.

'Four,' he said as an older woman walked out from behind him. There was no introduction needed as the family resemblance was apparent. With the same fair hair and brilliant blue eyes as Finn and his girls, this had to be his mother.

'What brings you all here?' It seemed a tad out of character for him to bring his entire family to her doorstep when he'd been concerned about keeping his daughters at a distance from her lest they got too close. Even more so when she hadn't heard from him for a while.

'The girls wanted to come to the beach. I… er…didn't know you'd be here.' He looked as though he'd been caught red-handed doing something he shouldn't, but he'd been to her house and knew she lived only a few metres away.

She frowned, not quite understanding what they were all doing here or how she was supposed to act around them. Especially when his mother was here too. Whilst she doubted Finn had shared anything about the time they had spent together, she couldn't be sure what he had told her about the nature of their relationship. He certainly appeared uncomfortable to have run into her on her home turf.

'It is a small town, I guess.' She was at a loss as to why he was being so cool with her now. Yes, it was awkward meeting for the first time after they'd had sex, and having his mother and children witness it, but as far as she was aware she hadn't done anything to warrant getting the cold shoulder. Given the nature of his recent messages, she had assumed they were going to continue seeing each other at least. Now she wasn't so sure.

'We're going to get ice cream. Daddy said we can have strawberry sauce and chocolate sprinkles if we're good.' Niamh's enthusiasm for the treat made it seem likely it was her sole reason for suggesting this particular location. It might have been more comfortable for Finn if he had simply taken them to an ice cream parlour from the outset.

'You're lucky girls to have such a lovely daddy. Enjoy your ice cream.' She extricated herself from the girls' grasp and, with an uncertain smile for Finn, she began to walk away.

'Can Lily come too, Daddy?'

'What's your favourite ice cream, Lily?'

Niamh, then Maeve, blocked her escape route, closely followed by their grandmother, who stepped in front of Finn, who seemed temporarily struck dumb by the situation they'd found themselves in.

'Yes, do come with us. The girls have been talking about you non-stop since you called to the house. I'm Finn's mother, Josie, by the way, since he hasn't bothered to introduce us.' The elegant older woman's smile was welcoming and friendly, unlike her son's at this current moment.

'Lily Riordan. It's lovely to meet you.'

'I've told you Lily's a very busy woman, Mum. I'm sure she has better things to do than get ice cream with us.'

It was the look of disappointment on the girls' faces as much as Finn's attempt to get rid of her which made Lily contradict him. 'I'm never too busy for ice cream, and I would love a mint choc chip. What's your favourite flavour?' She took the girls' hands and walked towards the ice cream van she knew would be sitting in the car park nearby for all the beach-goers.

'Strawberry.'

'Chocolate. That's Daddy's favourite too, but Granny likes boring old vanilla,' Niamh shared along the way.

'Everyone has different tastes. If we all did the same things all the time life would be boring. I mean, sometimes you want something you probably shouldn't have and that's okay too.' Lily spoke loud enough for Finn to hear too and she hoped that he would pick up on her allusion to guilty pleasures. Perhaps that was what she was to him and she didn't care as long as he would tell her what was bothering him. Not knowing what was going on in his head was as bad as being ghosted.

'Why don't you and Charlie go and get us a seat and the girls and I will get the ice creams?' It was Josie who gave them the space to talk and Lily wondered how much she knew. If Finn's thunderous expression was anything to go by, probably not a lot, she imagined.

They walked in silence over to the only picnic table which wasn't occupied by ice-cream-covered children and fussing adults yet.

She wanted to get straight to the point

rather than tiptoeing around the subject when they only had a limited amount of time alone.

'Are you regretting what happened the other night?'

Finn flinched then glanced behind him as though worried someone had heard. It didn't bode well for their future as a couple.

'No…not exactly. It's just…the girls being here…it's making things awkward.'

'They don't have to be. All right, neither of us was ready for a meet-the-parent scenario, but it's not the end of the world. I've met your girls before, and all we're doing is having an ice cream together. If you want me to leave, I'll go before they come back.' She didn't want an accidental meeting to spoil what they had together when she was so looking forward to the next time they got to be alone.

Finn stretched out across the table and grabbed her arm before she could go. 'That's not what I meant, not what I want.'

'No? What is it you do want then?' She was finding it hard to swallow, her mouth suddenly dry as he looked at her with that same predatory hunger she'd seen on his face before.

'You.'

It was the answer she'd hoped for, yet it still made her insides flip as though she were on a big dipper. She'd never needed a man to want her as much as Finn, simply because she'd never needed one as much. That look in his eye, the tight grip on her arm and the longing in his voice were confirmation that their time together hadn't been a one-off.

They both wanted to do it all over again.

CHAPTER EIGHT

Finn swore under his breath. With Lily looking at him the way she had the other morning in her bed and his family coming towards him, he was torn over how to act. All he wanted to do was take her somewhere private and kiss her senseless. Well, more than that, but neither of them were exhibitionists. Instead, he let go of her arm before either the girls or his mum saw and got their hopes up.

'We got mint choc chip for you, Lily,' Niamh announced proudly as her ice cream melted over her fingers.

'Thank you so much.' Lily beamed, taking the proffered treat.

Finn took his from Maeve, who didn't seem as enthusiastic as her sister in the delivery.

'They were fighting over who got to give

Lily her ice cream,' his mother explained, as if there were any logic involved. She gave him a knowing look, suggesting there was more going on than sibling rivalry. He had to look away, sure she would see right through him as well and realise that he and Lily were more than work colleagues too.

'Why don't we go for a walk to the park and eat these on the way?' He was already on his feet, unable to watch Lily licking her scoop of mint choc chip without his imagination going into lewd overdrive.

The girls didn't need much persuading but his sudden request did draw questioning eyebrows from his mother and Lily. Nevertheless they acquiesced and soon formed a short crocodile walking in single file along the narrow pathway leading to the play area, with Finn bringing up the rear.

'I can make some excuse and leave you all to it if you want.' Without drawing the attention of the others, Lily had slowed her pace and hung back to speak to him.

'Why would I want that?'

She rolled her eyes at him. 'It's kind of obvious you're uncomfortable with me being here. Admit it.'

'Yes, I'm uncomfortable, but not for the reasons you think.' As soon as he saw an opening he took it. With his mum occupied supervising the girls, who'd run ahead to go on the climbing frame, he grabbed Lily's hand and pulled her into the trees lining their route.

'What are you doing?' She laughed as he backed her up against an oak tree whose thick bushy branches provided sufficient camouflage to keep them hidden from view.

'What I've wanted to do from the moment we saw you. From the second I left your bed.' He captured her mouth with his, greedily drinking her in like a man who'd just been given water after a month in the desert.

'In here? Really?' She laughed again as he began kissing her neck, his body already on fire for her.

Lily's giggle did little to dissuade him from letting his libido rule his head.

'We'll have to be quiet or we'll end up the talk of the town,' he muttered against her skin, with no intention of keeping quiet.

There was something about being with Lily which made him reckless and gave him the same adrenaline rush as running headlong into a fire. It was exciting and dangerous and he couldn't seem to give it up, despite the risks.

'Yeah. Oh, look, your ice cream is melting.' Lily leaned over and licked the stream of liquid chocolate running down his hand, and he knew having a physical relationship would be easier than not having her in his life at all. And infinitely more enjoyable.

'Sod the ice cream,' he said, taking her cone and tossing it, along with his, onto the grass so he could take her properly in his arms and kiss her thoroughly enough to prove himself worthy of her.

She tasted fresh and minty, her tongue cold in his mouth, but everything about her was making him hot. He knew he had to put the brakes on before they careered completely out of control.

'Sex in a public place is probably not something two forty-something pillars of the community should be doing.'

'Hmm, but it feels so good.' She reached

down and took a firm hold of his burgeoning erection, to make him groan.

'You're trouble, you know that, Tiger Lily?' He took a step back and adjusted himself so he could be seen in public again without being arrested for lewd behaviour.

She pulled him back for a quick peck on the lips before making her way back onto the path. 'Yeah, but you can't keep away from me, can you?'

No. No, he couldn't.

Lily couldn't believe he'd done that. Not that she was complaining when she was almost skipping along the path like a teenager. Finn made her feel like that. Carefree, that nothing mattered except being with him. It was dangerous, she knew that, but she figured she was due a little fun. A sexy interlude to boost her ego couldn't do any harm as long as they kept things casual. It was bound to fizzle out eventually. This scorching passion they'd ignited couldn't burn for ever, but she would fan the flames until there was nothing but ashes left between them.

'Hey, girls. It was lovely to see you again

but I'm going to head home. Thanks for the ice cream.' She caught up with the rest of the family to make her excuses and felt a little guilty when they begged her to stay. Then she caught Finn's gaze again, that blatant want reflected so brightly it turned her insides molten, and she couldn't wait to get away. To be somewhere private, where they didn't have to hide what it was they wanted from each other. Physically, at least. She was trying to block out how much she was emotionally investing in him because it would spoil everything.

''Bye.' Lily waved to Niamh and Maeve, whose interest had now been captured by the recently vacated swings.

As she passed Finn she whispered, 'You know where I live,' and walked away. A little hip sway with every step because she knew he was watching her and couldn't resist teasing him the way he'd done with her, kissing her when he knew they couldn't do anything more without risking being seen.

She'd barely had time to take her coat off and freshen up at home before he was ringing her bell.

'That was quick. Won't the girls wonder where you are?'

'Mum's taking them back to her house to bake cupcakes. I'll suffer the consequences of their sugar high later, but it's worth it if I get to spend time with you.' He didn't wait for an invitation, pushing her back inside and closing the door with his foot.

'Careful, it's beginning to sound as though you like me,' she teased, glad that his awkwardness around her hadn't been because he was growing tired of her already. Quite the opposite when he couldn't seem to get enough of her, already kissing the side of her neck, hitting all her erogenous zones at once.

'Hmm, maybe a little bit.' He was nibbling that little bit of skin just behind her ear which undid her every time and sliding his hand up under her dress.

She let out a helpless sigh, unsure how long her legs were going to hold her up if he continued to wreak havoc on her body. 'Do you want to take this into the bedroom?'

'I'm good here. You were right, it's nice to try something different every once in a while.' He flipped her round so she was facing into the wall as he hitched her dress up and pulled her panties down, cold air hitting her naked backside.

Finn pushed up against her so she could feel the hard bulge in his jeans-clad crotch and a tsunami of arousal crashed through her body, obliterating everything but the need to have him.

'Finn—' It was a plea to show her some mercy, to relieve the ache pulsing in every part of her. She was relinquishing control of her body, trusting him to take care of her.

'I want you so much, Lily,' he whispered deep in her ear, turning her on to the point her clothes felt too restrictive. It was a relief when he released her from the fabric prison, cupping her breasts in his hands, rolling and pulling her taut nipples until she was grinding her body back against his, trying to drive him to the brink of insanity with her.

The sound of him unzipping his fly signalled her victory. A short-lived triumph as he slid his fingers between her thighs and into her wet core. Lily moaned as he stroked her, his fingers filling her, stretching her, taking control of her orgasm. He brought her there quickly and she had to brace herself against the wall as it slammed into her.

There was no time to come down from that high as Finn nudged her legs apart and pushed into her with a quick thrust.

There was a time and place for slow and gentle and one for plain old lust. They were both ready for something different.

She'd convinced him a fling was the way to go because she knew that was all he could give her. A good time. And boy, did he.

She was beginning to want more of an emotional connection, more of a relationship and more of Finn. But for now she would take what he was giving her. Absolute pleasure.

His hands were on her hips as he pounded into her, his breath quickening in her ear as he drove them both over the edge. Finn slammed his hand against the wall as he released the full extent of his desire inside her with a groan.

If a physical relationship was all that was on offer she would grab it with both hands when it made her feel so good. Sure, there would be a time when she was alone again with only memories to keep her warm at night, but it was preferable to the life she'd had before Finn had shown her what she'd been missing.

A husband, a family and good health might not be in her future, but she would settle for an unbelievable sex life and whatever time she could get with this man who reminded her she was alive every time he touched her.

She turned around and he kissed her, his tongue softly stroking hers a contrast to the fast and furious lovemaking of only moments ago. She wasn't averse to either and his seemingly insatiable appetite for her, at least on this base level, was enough to convince her that this was enough. For now.

How was he ever going to give this up? The thought of never holding Lily again, kissing her, making love to her, was something he didn't want to contemplate. Yet by the very nature of the arrangement they'd entered into, this couldn't last for ever.

'Well, that was certainly different.' His voice was as shaky as the rest of him following their encounter. Lily made him feel things, experience things he'd never had before. This passion, this fire was something rare, he knew that, but it was also something they'd found together.

Only time would tell if it would burn itself out or blaze like wildfire, out of control and a threat to life. His.

Lily flashed him a grin as they fixed their clothes. 'Good different?'

'Definitely. I mean, I'm not sure these old bones would hold up to doing this all the time…'

'Trust me, you've still got the moves.' She chuckled, shaking her head.

He had to admit the ego boost was nice, but it had a lot to do with his partner too. When he was with her his age didn't matter because she had given him a new lease of life. One he was enjoying and couldn't see without her in it.

'Do you want to go for a coffee or a walk or something?' It seemed backwards to ask her out now after what they'd done together, but it would have been cold to simply zip up his trousers and leave. Besides, he wasn't ready to be without her company just yet.

'Sure. Let me get my coat.' Lily had studied him for a moment before she answered, as though she was trying to figure out if it was a genuine offer. It was disappointing that she doubted his sincerity. He'd agreed to this casual arrangement to prevent any sort of relationship interfering in his home life, but that didn't mean he was merely using her for sex. Despite it being Lily's idea, he didn't think that was all she was getting out of it either. If that was the case she wouldn't even have entertained the idea of coming along with the family today. She liked the girls and he was pretty sure she liked him for more than his middle-aged body too.

Lily's bungalow was right on the edge of the shore. The perfect place to get some fresh air and a head clear of all thoughts of the bedroom. Or the hallway, or the number of places he could quite happily make love to Lily. It was important for her to know this was about more than sex to him, even if he couldn't afford a serious emotional entanglement.

'It's peaceful here. No screaming or crying or endless questions.' Finn loved his daughters but there was very rarely any quiet time to be found. Work too was a constant source of noise. Even when they weren't dealing with an emergency call, the station was full of men clattering around.

Lily smiled. 'Well, I don't have two young children bending my ear but I still enjoy being out here. It's as though nothing else matters and you can simply let the sound of the sea wash over you. Sorry, is that too tragic?'

'Not at all. I get it. Sometimes it's nice not to have to think about anything and just be. I never did go in for the partying and clubbing, or the need to be living it up all the time. I always enjoyed the quiet life.'

It might sound boring to some, but it had meant more to him spending time with Sara than being out on the town. Some men might have gone back out on the single scene after losing their wife, but that had never been more important to him than spending time with his children. That was why he'd never expected to meet another woman. This thing with Lily had taken him completely by surprise and he was still trying to process the implications of that when she was such a big part of his life now.

'I have to admit, I was the party girl when I was younger. Probably because I didn't think I had a long-term future and I thought I should experience everything life had to offer, all at once. I studied hard but I played harder. Never settling in one place too long with anyone in case something happened. There was no one to intervene. By that point I'd lost my mum too. Now I'm all about the quiet life, content to see out my days picking sea glass off the shore on my down time.' She bent down and stood back up, clutching a tiny speck of dark blue glass he would never have spotted in such a vast, stony expanse.

'Part of an old perfume bottle,' she exclaimed, as though she'd just discovered the Crown Jewels lying on her front doorstep.

'I can see you as a wild child, drinking shots and going to foam parties back in the day.'

'Hey, I could still do all that. If I wanted to.'

They were grinning at each other, but Finn knew there was an undercurrent of 'what if?' beneath their admissions. What could have happened if they'd met each other at that time? He didn't regret his life before her, he'd loved Sara and had his girls as a result, but there might have been a point when the timing would have been right for him and Lily. Where a proper relationship could have been possible.

'I never wanted to. Sara and I were childhood sweethearts. Getting married and having children is what's expected when you're together so long. I dare say it had something to do with me losing my father at such a young age too. I never knew him but the loss created a need for that stability of a family around me.' Whereas in Lily's case she had actively pushed against the idea because of the way hers had been taken so tragically from her.

'It's funny how these things shape you, influence the decisions you make.' The sad note in her voice and her wavering smile suggested there was nothing remotely funny about the choices she'd been forced to make as a result of her childhood. He couldn't help but pull her in for a hug. Although he was swamped with them daily from his girls, he was sure it was a long time since Lily had one.

She folded easily into his arms and they

stood on the beach for a while, his head resting on top of hers as the waves continued to crash in around them.

It wasn't until much later that he realised anyone could have seen them. The more startling realisation was that he didn't care, because in that moment a hug was what both of them had needed more than anything.

CHAPTER NINE

'So, you can rest assured if you ever have to deal with a cardiac emergency you are not on your own. Either the ambulance service or the fire brigade will be there to assist you.' Lily climbed down from the podium to a round of applause. She and Finn were still on their PR campaign, this time in the local high school, informing the younger generation of what to do in case of an emergency.

Finn stepped up to the microphone again, after already giving his talk on fire safety, and now came the dreaded Q and A session. In her experience of these things, most teenagers were too embarrassed to ask further questions in front of their classmates and those curious enough to do so were inevitably teased mercilessly about being a swot.

'Thank you, Dr Riordan. Now, does anyone have any questions?'

A few titters and mumbled voices sounded in the assembly hall before one brave, sassy student called out, 'Do you do hen parties?'

Ever the professional, Finn answered, 'Only if they're on fire.'

The headmaster walked forward at that point to glare daggers at the group of young girls who appeared to have taken a shine to the mature fireman, and Lily couldn't blame them when she was completely smitten with him too.

'I think that will do for today. Thank you, Mr Finnegan and Dr Riordan.' He began a round of applause and Lily was relieved their little presentation was over for another day.

A member of the Parent Teacher Association who had asked them to speak today led them to the staffroom, where they were honoured with tea and biscuits.

'I'm sorry about that little outburst. Teenagers and their hormones, eh?'

Finn looked a tad embarrassed as the matter of his fan club was raised by one of the ruddy-cheeked members of the PTA hovering with her cup of tea in hand.

'No harm done,' he mumbled and sipped at his tea.

'There's something about a man in uniform that makes us all a bit giddy.' She winked at Finn before she took off again and Lily nearly spat out her own tea.

'We really should see about setting up a proper fan club for you. Maybe even get a calendar printed. I'm sure it would make a lot of money for charity, judging by the number of female admirers you seem to attract.' Lily was teasing him but she was suffering from an attack of jealousy jabbing sharply at her insides. Seeing other women fawn over him was a reminder that she had no real claim on him when their relationship was a nonstarter. She was nothing more than his goodtime girl, and who knew that would last if someone else came along who could offer him more than an uncertain future?

It was her own fault that he saw her now as nothing more than his secret lover when she had been the one to suggest it. At the time it had seemed the only way to keep him in her life, but the longer they spent together the more she yearned for something more. The co-operative between their departments meant they were working closer than ever, which was as frustrating as it was enjoyable when she couldn't touch him or kiss him for fear of being discovered. She didn't know how long she could continue being someone's dirty secret.

As far as any of the residents knew, Finn was a widower and available. Even now there was a group of the mums whispering in the corner and shooting furtive admiring glances in his direction, probably wondering if they stood a chance with him. Lily was so insecure about the nature of their relationship even she couldn't be sure.

Her paranoia was interrupted by the bushy-haired school secretary rushing into the room. 'Headmaster, there's an incident with one of the students. She's on the roof and refusing to come down.'

There was a clatter of china as everyone abandoned their tea to go and investigate, including Lily and Finn. They stood in the playground with the group of children who had also gathered, staring up at the small figure standing on the edge of the roof.

'That's Ruth Harlow. What on earth is she doing up there?' The headmaster, though clearly concerned for her safety, seemed more annoyed than sympathetic with the young girl.

'I've phoned for the emergency services. Apparently she was very upset today during PE. I think she's been told she can no longer take part in competitive sports.'

Recognition dawned deep in the pit of Lily's stomach. 'She's one of my patients. I had to give her the bad news this week. Let me go and talk to her.'

Ruth had been upset when she was advised her heart condition was going to limit her sporting activities and Lily had referred her for counselling, as well as making future appointments to check in on her. Apparently that hadn't been enough to look after her mental health.

'You're not going up there, Lily.' Finn's command was unexpected and unwanted, making her hackles rise as he tried to tell her what to do.

'She's upset. I know what it's like to have to live with an illness limiting and controlling your life. I'm just going to go up and sit with her until the emergency services get here. She shouldn't be on her own.'

Lily went to move and Finn grabbed her by the wrist.

'I don't want you to overdo it by climbing up there. That's my department.'

She prised his fingers from her arm. 'I know my limits, Finn, and I know my job. You have no say in my life. After all, it's not like we're in a serious relationship or anything.'

His mouth tightened but he didn't argue with her. How could he? There was little point pretending there was more to their relationship than just sex because he wanted to pull rank.

'At least let me come up with you,' he insisted as the caretaker brought over a ladder and propped it against the wall.

'Fine, but keep your distance. I don't want you to interfere.' Lily began her ascent up the ladder, cursing her choice of dress and heels, which were totally inappropriate for climbing, especially with Finn following close behind.

'Ruth? It's Lily Riordan. I'm just coming to check you're okay.' She tentatively stepped over to the edge of the roof where Ruth was now sitting, her legs dangling over the edge. A glance back told her that Finn was close but still managing to give them some space and privacy.

'It's not fair,' Ruth cried, shuffling closer to the edge.

'I know, sweetheart. You don't know this, but I have a heart condition myself. I had to stop competing in sports too, and I know it seems like the end of the world now but you will adapt.' There was no choice, other than to spend the rest of your days bemoaning the fact you'd been dealt a rotten hand in life. Something she had done for a while before deciding medicine was the new route she was going to take.

'I'm not good at anything else. Stupid heart. Why does it have to be me?'

'I can't answer that, but you're not alone. I'm sure we can find you some support groups, with people your age who have the same condition for you to talk to.'

Sometimes it made all the difference to simply get your worries off your chest. Despite her current beef with Finn, she was glad she'd confided in him about her illness and her fears rather than internalising it all and feeling worse. She had been annoyed that he'd tried to use her condition as an excuse to wrap her in cotton wool, but in hindsight it was nice to have someone who cared about her.

'It sucks.'

'It does, but it doesn't have to rule your life. There'll be other hobbies and interests, I promise you. We'll do everything we can at the hospital to help you live as normal a life as possible.'

'I didn't know you had a heart condition too.'

'See? With treatment it can be managed and no one has to know. Hopefully, with a few adjustments, you can live as normal a life as possible. I will do everything I can to help you.'

The irony wasn't lost on Lily about the

manner of their conversation, advising some-one else about not letting their illness define them. She ought to take a leaf out of her own book and the advice of a certain fire-man standing not too far away about living in the moment instead of getting bogged down in her fears about the future. And Lily only wished her sister had been given the same opportunities her patients had these days.

'Promise?' Ruth looked up at her with big trusting eyes.

'I promise.' She crossed her heart, vowing to Ruth and herself to help her through this difficult time.

Ruth looked down at the assembled crowd. 'I didn't mean to cause a fuss. I just wanted somewhere quiet to go so I could think straight.'

'Don't worry. Everyone will be glad you're safe. That's all any of us want. Now, can we get down? I'm not very good with heights.'

Ruth attempted to get to her feet but slipped on the loose gravel lining the roof. She landed with a thump before Lily could get to her.

'What…what happened?' Now disorientated, Ruth was lying on her back. She touched the top of her scalp and flinched when she saw the blood dripping down her fingers.

'You've had a fall. Don't try to get up. I need to take a look at you.' Lily didn't want to panic her, but the blood from her head injury was quickly turning the gravel around her deep scarlet.

As she parted the teenager's hair gently she could see the wound, deep enough to warrant a couple of stitches, but that wasn't the main concern. Lily knew the girl was on anti-coagulant drugs for her condition, which meant her blood wouldn't clot. It explained the vast pool of blood spreading out to stain the gravel like a gothic halo around her head.

'My head hurts.' Ruth reached up again, but Lily stopped her from touching the injury site.

'You've had quite a knock, but I don't want you getting that wound infected. We have to stop the bleeding so I need to put pressure on it, okay? It might hurt a little.'

Ruth nodded and Lily reminded her to try not to move. She was afraid there could be other damage apart from the superficial.

Apart from neck or spinal damage, there was a chance she could have a subdural haematoma, blood on the brain, which could require surgery.

'Finn?' she yelled, knowing he wouldn't be too far away.

He was at her side in seconds.

'What happened?'

'Ruth slipped and hit her head. Can you get an ambulance here? In the meantime, I'm going to need a cold compress and a first aid kit with dressing and bandages to try and stop the bleeding.'

He didn't even take time to answer before he was off in search of the required items.

It was a positive sign that her patient was alert and talking, her breathing apparently normal. However, as she was losing so much blood there was a chance of Ruth going into shock with her vital organs not getting enough oxygen. She needed to elevate the girl's legs to improve the blood supply, but there was nothing around to prop her up and she needed to keep applying pressure to the head injury.

Thankfully, Finn turned up in record time

with everything she needed and more. 'What can I do to help?'

Lily could have kissed him there and then. 'We need to keep her warm and lift her legs up to get the blood circulating sufficiently around her body.'

'I brought some blankets. They should do the job.' He tossed the first aid kit over before covering Ruth with one of the blankets he'd commandeered. The second one he rolled up to prop under her legs. Then he helped her dress the wound.

'We make a good team,' she told him, her feelings for him swelling so deep inside her she might just explode. He was there when she needed him at work. If only the same could be said out of hours. She only got to see him when he wasn't occupied by his other priorities.

'That we do.' He was looking at her exactly the way she wanted him to, until her insides were melting and her brain was playing a montage of their best bits.

It was obvious she was falling in love with this man, probably even to Ruth, who was lying between them watching their interplay with a knowing smile. She likely imagined this to be some romantic fantasy where they'd found love and were about to live happily ever after. But as much as Lily wanted her patient to have a normal life, it was probably too late to have one herself.

It took the paramedics some manoeuvring to get Ruth safely into the back of the ambulance, leaving Lily and Finn to make their own way down again.

She made the mistake of looking over the end of the roof and completely froze. 'Finn? I can't move.'

Her feet felt as though they were cemented to the roof, her heart was racing and her vision was blurry, the ground seeming to rush up to meet her.

'It's fine. I've got you.'

He walked over and took her hand. Lily buried her head in his chest, afraid that one wrong move would have her plummeting to the ground.

'Only you would come up onto a roof to save someone else even though you're afraid of heights.' He wasn't mocking her, his voice low and soothing.

'I don't think I can get back down.'

'I'm here for you,' he said, releasing her from his embrace to coax her over towards the ladder.

She took several unsteady steps as he led her by the hand, but she couldn't find it in her to set foot on the first rung. 'I can't do it.'

'Okay, you asked me to trust that you knew how to do your job, now I'm asking you to do the same.' All of a sudden he was bundling her over his shoulder as though she weighed nothing at all.

Lily let out a startled scream. 'What if you drop me?'

'I won't. You'll have to trust me.'

That was half of Lily's problem. She'd spent so long on her own it was difficult for her to trust anyone not to hurt her, either emotionally or by dropping her head first from a school building. If they were ever going to have anything more than a meaningless fling she knew she had to open her heart and trust he wasn't going to do her harm.

'Okay, but don't expect me to keep my eyes open.'

That made him laugh as he slowly and carefully walked the two of them back down to solid ground. The round of applause from the spectating pupils and teachers still watching let her know when it was safe to look again.

If it wasn't for all the eyes upon them and Finn's need to keep her secret, she would've kissed him. Instead she had to settle for a simple thank you. Any further gratitude would have to wait until they were in private again.

Finn wanted to kiss her stupid and make her promise never to scare him like that again, but it wasn't in keeping with the nature of their relationship. He'd already ticked her off by crossing the line to express his concern about her going up there. Thank goodness he'd been there and she'd put her faith in him to get her back down again.

It was proving tricky to keep his feelings at bay for Lily when she evoked so many in him. So much for keeping things casual when he was already so invested in what happened to her.

'You should let the paramedics check you over.'

Lily tutted. 'I'm fine. Just a case of the wobbles. It's you who probably needs pain relief after carrying me all that way.'

He gave her a sideways glance that he hoped conveyed his annoyance at her for talking about herself that way again. It seemed to do the trick as she simply smiled at him and made no further reference to her weight.

'You had a shock. I want to make sure you're all right, that's all.'

'And I appreciate it, but I'm fine. I've been looking after myself for a long time.'

Finn got the impression she was telling him to back off, that his concern was straying beyond the boundaries of a no-strings fling, but he couldn't help himself. He didn't want anything bad to happen to Lily. He cared for her. Perhaps more than he'd be willing to admit, or than was appropriate for their arrangement. He was in deep and trying to keep her at arm's length wasn't working out so far.

It only made him want to be with her more.

CHAPTER TEN

'I'M…GOING…TO…have…to…go,' Finn repeated in between snatched kisses as he tried again to back out of the door. Although it was very tempting to stay when Lily only had a sheet to cover her naked body. Something which only a short time ago they had both been wrapped up in.

'It's torture watching you walk out this door every time we get five minutes together,' she said, clutching the sheet to her chest, her hair still mussed from their time in her bed.

'I'd like to think it was more than five minutes, but I hear what you're saying. It would be nice to actually spend the whole night together, instead of me sneaking over in between shifts and the school run.'

It was exhausting juggling this double life,

yet he didn't want to give any of it up. His family, work and Lily were all important to him, but they were all separate entities demanding his time. When he wasn't working the night shift he was splitting his time between being with the girls or Lily.

It was almost as if he were having an illicit affair, lying about where he was so he could jump into bed with his lover, even though he didn't have a wife to cheat on. Lily had been great about the whole thing, understanding about his need to protect his children and spending quality time with them. Keeping things casual had been her idea for that very reason, but it wasn't fair on her either.

A fling was a compromise so they could be together without putting any expectations on each other, but he didn't feel good about simply walking away from her after they had sex. As though he was simply using her, when the connection they had was much deeper than purely physical.

'I don't see what alternative we have.' Lily sighed. 'Unless you're talking about breaking up?'

'No, of course not.' His response was automatic because the last thing he wanted was to lose her when being with her was the best thing that had happened to him in a year.

Since being with Lily, he'd rediscovered himself again and an enjoyment in being alive rather than merely enduring it for the sake of his children. It made him want to be with her even more and there was only one way he could have that without detracting from his other responsibilities.

'What if we move things on from our casual status?' He closed the door again, prepared to at least give the conversation the extra time it deserved.

'What do you mean?'

'I mean, I'm enjoying the sex, and being with you, but not the sneaking around.'

'Really? I thought that was what's making it exciting for you. You know, having sex when and where we can manage it. In the cab of the fire engine when the rest of your crew are asleep was my particular favourite.' She was grinning at him with that same naughty glint in her eye she'd had when she'd turned up at the station that night wearing little more than her lingerie under her overcoat.

Under the guise of discussing their 'project', they'd steamed up the windows of the rig that night after a whole twenty-four hours apart. It seemed they simply couldn't get enough of one another, and that wasn't easy to manage when they had so little time together.

Lord help him, but he was reaching for her again. Getting the requisite eight hours of sleep didn't seem so important when she was slowly unfurling that sheet to give him a glimpse of everything he would be leaving behind simply so he could be in his own bed when his girls woke up.

'Trust me, there hasn't been a single moment with you I haven't enjoyed, but I want to do everything.' He took his jacket off again before pulling Lily back to him.

'Everything?' she asked, eyebrows raised.

'Everything. Dinner, walks along the beach, vegging out in front of the TV. All the usual things couples do when they're together.' He hitched her legs up around his waist and carried her back towards the bedroom.

'So we're a couple now? I thought you were trying to avoid that.' With her arms wrapped around his neck, she was kissing her way along his jawline and nibbling on his earlobe. Doing everything she could to test his restraint. Not that she needed to when he was a willing participant.

'Yeah, well, I'm getting greedy where you're concerned. How about it? You want to go steady with me?' He was teasing to cover his own anxiety surrounding the question.

It was a big step for him to commit to something more with Lily. Though it had been her suggestion to keep things casual, he'd agreed in order to protect his girls. He worried that if they got too close to Lily and things didn't work out it would be his fault, but they couldn't keep hiding for ever. The only way they could spend real quality time together was if they brought everything out into the open, but that would entail a commitment neither of them had signed on for. It would mean being more to one another than bed buddies because he would only risk his family's wellbeing if he thought they could make it as a couple.

He set Lily carefully onto the bed and waited for her answer. It was only then he realised she might be the one to end things if she didn't want their situation to get any more serious than their need for frequent sexual release.

'Are you sure? What about the girls? I know you didn't want them to get confused about what was going on between us, and you're already aware of my medical situation.' She was reminding him that more was involved than waking up together in the same house or having family meals together.

'Dilated cardiomyopathy—I know, I've been looking into it. I know you lost your father and sister suddenly, but you've had a warning. You've got time to make whatever changes are going to be necessary to keep you around for a lot longer. I read you can get a pacing device to regulate your heart.'

It had been on his mind for a while, knowing he was falling deeper for Lily every day. He'd wanted to look beyond what she was telling him, what she believed, to see what *could* happen. So they could all be prepared.

'Someone's been doing their research, but it's no guarantee that the same thing that happened to the rest of my family won't happen to me. Are you really willing to take the chance that some day I might simply drop dead too?'

Lily was being brutal about her own possible demise, but Finn knew it was a defence mechanism. She was trying to put him off the idea of getting into a proper relationship in case he did change his mind further down the line and hurt her as a result. He knew because he had the same worry.

The only way they were going to get through this was to think logically instead of basing their future on fear. There was treatment available, if and when Lily needed it. They could both stop using her illness as an excuse not to get close to one another. The time had come for him to open his heart again and stop being afraid that history was going to repeat itself. Lily was the most vibrant, clever woman he'd ever met and so far there had been no indication that there was anything wrong with her other than that same terror he harboured of losing another loved one.

'We're all going to die some time, Tiger Lily. In the meantime, we should make the most of the life we do have. That's not to say we have to rush things, we can just take it one day at a time and let the girls get used to having you around before we make any grand announcement.' Daddy having a girlfriend could cause all kinds of hysteria. Either they would love it or hate it and he'd prefer to build up to it gradually rather than shock them with this big change in their lives.

'I think we can manage that. Let's say dinner or even a night at the cinema the next time you're free?'

'It's a date. Until then, perhaps we can have a little more *casual* fun,' he said, pulling his shirt back over his head and climbing onto the bed with her.

'I thought you needed to get home for some proper sleep?' Lily shuffled in against him with no apparent intention of letting him go again.

'It's overrated. I can think of much better ways to spend my time,' he said, suddenly finding a new burst of energy.

'I know I said you should live your own life, Mum, but you're not giving me much notice.

I have to get to work for my shift.' He was already running behind today after staying over at Lily's this morning and being late getting the girls to school. His mum was the only one who could babysit and without her he was lost. This was stress he did not need.

'I'm sure Lily would help if you asked her. She's such a nice woman and the girls love her.'

If he didn't know better he'd swear his mother was engineering this for Lily to spend more time with his daughters. They hadn't discussed it but he got the impression his mother knew there was something going on between him and Lily and she was trying to push it further.

'Daddy, Niamh is all wet.' Little Maeve was tugging on his shirt, trying to get attention, and he just knew there had been some catastrophe in another room. At least it was a distraction from his mother's matchmaking plans. He knew Lily would come if he asked, but it would be taking their relationship to a new level by getting her to help with his daughters. It could prove too much too soon for all involved. Yet he wasn't sure what choice he had at this moment in time.

'I'll have to go, Mum. You have fun and I'll talk to you tomorrow. I'll sort something out here, don't worry.' He ended the call, trying to sound positive for his mother's benefit even though he had been left in a real bind. That was the thing about trying to do everything on his own, he had no one else to turn to for help.

The sound of glass smashing sounded from the kitchen.

'Niamh? Don't move. I'm coming.' He rushed in to see her rubbing her eyes, standing in the middle of the room, water, glass and juice all around her.

'I was just trying to get a drink, Daddy.' Her bottom lip began to quiver and Finn gathered her up before the tears began to fall.

'I know, sweetheart. We'll go and get you cleaned up. Maeve, don't go into the kitchen until I get all the glass swept up, okay?'

'I know you have to go to work, Daddy. I wanted to show you I could look after me and Maeve if Granny can't come.' She was clinging onto his neck as he carried her to the bathroom, clearly stressing about his problems. At her age she shouldn't have to be taking on the responsibility of her younger sister and he knew it was a reflection of his struggles since losing their mum. It was about time he opened up and let someone in again, for their sake as well as his own.

He thought about Lily and everything they had shared in the early hours of the morning. She had agreed to venture into something more than they already had together, but he wondered if asking for her help now was overstepping the mark.

In an ideal world he and Lily would be perfectly suited, she'd fit easily into the girls' lives and they'd all live happily ever after. The reality could prove somewhat different. She had her reasons for not wanting anything serious and had gone to great lengths to ensure she didn't have anyone in her life to worry about. It would be selfish of him therefore to expect her to slip into his family now because it suited him. Besides, only time would tell if he was truly ready to get into another relationship. They both had baggage they weren't keen to dump on the other.

However, this was an emergency and he was looking for a favour, not for her to sign adoption papers.

'Don't you worry about it. I'll phone a friend and see if I can get them to come over.'

'Lily? She could read us another story and stay for a sleepover.' Niamh was muffled as he stripped her wet nightdress over her head to dry her with a towel and give her some new PJs to put on.

It was funny that Lily was the first person to spring to his daughter's mind too. Although it could have been merely because she was the only person he had allowed into the house since Sara's death.

'We'll see. I'll have to phone her. You two brush your teeth.' He squeezed toothpaste onto their brushes and ushered them closer to the sink, while debating whether or not he should ask Lily for help.

There was no question that he wanted to see her again, even though he had to get to work, but he didn't want to be trying to rush them into something too soon. It was probably for the best if he did make out this was more of a favour he was asking of a friend in an emergency than a lead into their new relationship and keep them all in their comfort zone.

He called her number as he wandered into the kitchen to begin the clean-up of the mess his daughter had caused trying to prove she was able to fill the void her mother had left. It wasn't down to Niamh, or Lily, or anyone else to prove themselves as a replacement for the wife he had lost. Sara was gone and he had to move on with his life. Hopefully with Lily in it. If he didn't scare her off tonight.

He was simply in a predicament, and one that could easily be solved if he was brave enough to ask for help.

Lily walked in on a scene of chaos at Finn's place. When he answered the door he was holding Niamh's hand with Maeve on his back, her arms wrapped around his neck. He was carrying a bag full of rubbish with a mop tucked into his arm.

'Thank you so much for coming over.' The relief was palpable as she took the cleaning equipment from him to lighten his load.

She was glad he had thought to call on her

for assistance. It showed a trust in her she knew he didn't give easily and said a lot for their budding relationship. Although she was wary of it being too soon to be introduced to his daughters now as someone other than a friend of their daddy. For them and her.

She'd spent a lifetime safeguarding against this kind of thing happening, of getting close to people. Now, not only was she involved with Finn on a deeper level than either of them had expected, but she was insinuating herself into his family. His trust, his optimistic belief that they could work through all of their issues was heart-warming, but that could make it all the more painful if things went wrong. There was nothing she wanted more than to be with him, to have that normal life most people took for granted. Experience had taught her differently, so she remained cautious, and could only hope for the best when Finn was risking so much for her.

It was clear how much he'd loved Sara and that he would take a bullet if it meant protecting his kids. The fact he was willing to take a chance on her, on them, showed a faith in their relationship she prayed she could match.

'It's not a problem. I'm not on call tonight and spending the evening reading to your girls will be more fun than sitting in front of the TV on my own all night.' She'd been pleased to hear his voice on the phone, even if it was to ask her to babysit. He could have played it safe and kept her and his girls separate so as not to confuse matters, but he was taking the next step. The best thing she could do was take it with him.

Now she was here she knew she would love having some time with the children, getting to know them. It would bring her closer to Finn, the place she most liked to be.

'They can stay up for a little while and you can have my bed for the night.'

'Is your mum okay? I know she usually minds the girls for you.'

'To be honest, I think she needs a break. We've relied heavily on her this past year.'

'I'm sure she's loved every second being with her granddaughters. Now, Niamh, if it's all right with your dad, I've brought some stuff to make our own jewellery.' Lily wasn't going to simply put them to bed without any interaction, she wanted to make an effort with them. To show Finn she was willing to lower her defences to try and make this work too.

'Fine by me as long as no one ends up down at the station needing rings cut off because they're too tight and stopping the blood circulation.' He saw Lily's raised eyebrow. 'It happens.'

'I promise, no emergency visits to the fire station.'

Niamh swapped her father's hand for Lily's and Maeve clambered off her father's back to take her other hand, neither apparently having any misgivings about her being here in place of their grandmother.

'In that case I better get moving.' Finn kissed each of his daughters on the cheek and reached up and did the same with Lily. She hadn't expected any display of affection in front of the girls, and she wasn't sure they'd even seen the swift goodbye kiss, but it meant the world to her. He was ready to move on if she was and there was a chance for more than a fling with Finn, maybe even a life.

'What did you bring?'

'Can we see?'

The girls were tugging at the zip on the bag of materials she'd brought.

'We'll take it into the kitchen and spread everything out on the table so you can have a look.' With the last-minute plea for help she'd thrown some pieces of sea glass, craft wire and some necklace cord in her bag in the hope it would keep two small children entertained until bedtime.

She made sure to cover the table with some old newspapers so as not to ruin Finn's furniture with scores or scratches before emptying out her treasures. The girls, who had taken their seats at the table, were wide-eyed as the sparkling green and blue glass pieces tumbled out before them. To a small child they probably looked like precious jewels and when Lily found them glinting on the shore that was how they felt to her. In reality they were nothing more than chunks of bottles churned in the sea for decades until they were smooth, as she explained to the girls. Still, they turned the pieces of sea glass over in their fingers as though they were priceless.

'Go ahead, you can pick whatever colour you like.' Lily chose a small aquamarine piece, while Niamh went for a darker sapphire colour and Maeve clutched the large piece of deep green in her hand as though it were a real emerald.

Lily wound some of her craft wire around the sea glass to keep it secure, before adding jump rings for the cord to go through. She let the girls do that bit themselves, threading the pendant onto the necklace, so they were part of the process.

'Ta-dah!' She held her finished piece up for the girls to see but took a sudden rush of blood to the head, making her feel a little dizzy. It was probably low blood sugar, she concluded, since she had skipped dinner to get over here as soon as possible. Once the girls were in bed she would see if Finn had anything to eat in the fridge or even order a pizza.

'Are you okay, Lily?' Niamh watched her, a frown marring her forehead.

'I'm fine,' she replied with a smile, sorry she'd worried the child over nothing.

'Look at mine, Lily.' Thankfully little Maeve offered a distraction, holding up her chunky necklace for them to see.

'Good for you. Well done.' Lily helped fasten it around her neck and Maeve admired herself in the mirror after climbing down off her seat to get a better look.

'Can we make one for Daddy?' With her own necklace securely around her neck, Niamh was now choosing something for Finn.

'I'm not sure your daddy would be able to wear one to work. Why don't we make him a key ring instead?' Lily rummaged around in her bag of bits and pieces until she found a key ring fob. Knowing Finn, he wouldn't want to upset the girls and would wear the necklace to please them, but she could imagine the ribbing he would get from the other guys. At least a key ring was something practical.

Niamh pondered the idea for a moment before snatching up a frosted white piece of glass. 'I want to give him this one.'

'I want to help too.' Maeve came bounding over and selected another sizeable green bit.

'I've already picked Daddy's.' Niamh tried to elbow her sister out of the way, which prompted Maeve to push back. Lily knew she had to step in before their sibling rivalry got out of control and there were tears before bedtime. Finn would not be best pleased if his daughters went to bed upset.

'Why don't we put both on? There's enough room for two.' It might make the gift a bit clunky but she was sure he wouldn't mind.

She held out her hand to collect the two pieces they'd chosen and the girls managed to set aside their hostilities once more.

'You pick one too, Lily,' Niamh encouraged, the sweet way she was trying to involve Lily in their little project making her tear up.

How nice it would be to be part of this lovely family, enjoying time with the girls when Finn was working and spending nights with him when he wasn't. This was everything she could have wished for, but she worried that the spectre of her illness would eventually appear to spoil everything.

She could argue that their father would only want the gift to come from his girls but she didn't want to upset them. Once they were asleep she could always remove her contribution. So she picked out the rare piece of red from among the sea of blues and greens. It reminded her of Finn. The colour of his passion, and a one-off.

She focused on twisting the wire around the glass, making little cages to keep them protected and secure. If only there was such a thing for the heart, she wouldn't worry about getting close to this family in case it shattered.

As she hooked the last piece onto the key ring she experienced a momentary lapse of concentration, her brain seeming to switch off, causing a micro blackout. Nothing serious, but another reminder that she should get something to eat.

'Okay, girls, you'll need to take your necklaces off in bed but you can wear them tomorrow.' She wasn't going to take a chance on them getting tangled up in their sleep.

The pair groaned and reluctantly took off their new creations. Lily left them on the table beside the key ring for Finn in case they tried to sneak them on again in the middle of the night.

'Will you be here when we give Daddy his present?'

'I…er…don't know, Niamh, but I'm sure

he'll be thrilled when you give it to him.'
They hadn't discussed the morning's arrange-
ments so she didn't know if he wanted her
to stick around in order for him to get some
much-needed sleep, or go back to her own
house. In an ideal world she would get to
crawl into bed beside him for a cuddle, but
she knew they were a long way from doing
that when the girls were in the house.

The girls reluctantly left the table and Lily
stood up to go and tuck them in. That strange
light-headed sensation made her reach out
to steady herself on the table, only this time
it didn't go away. She was fighting to stay
on her feet, her body swaying on trembling
legs. The last thing she heard was the girls
calling out her name, then darkness swept in
and claimed her.

CHAPTER ELEVEN

FINN WAS PUTTING his stuff in his locker when his phone rang. Seeing it was his home number, he imagined it was Lily phoning for some advice on getting the girls to bed. No doubt they were running rings around her, completely hyper about having her to stay with them. He had a brief moment of panic in case there was something wrong, but he was sure if that had been the case she would have called him on her mobile.

'Hello? Lily? Is everything all right?'

'Daddy?'

Finn's heart dropped like a stone at the sound of his daughter's voice and his whole body went on high alert, anticipating bad news. Perhaps they hadn't got along as well as they had all expected after the last time and he'd rushed everything with Lily, upsetting the girls.

'Niamh? Where's Lily? What's happened?'

'Lily's asleep on the floor. I think she hit her head.'

Finn was already on his way back out of the door, signalling to his colleagues that he had to go. The only thing worse than hearing his daughter's frightened voice telling him Lily had had some accident was the sound of his youngest crying in the background. He should never have left them.

'Can you try and wake her, sweetheart?' He listened, phone wedged between his ear and his shoulder as he got into the car, hoping it was nothing too serious.

There was a bit of fumbling on the line and he could hear Niamh calling Lily's name. He could imagine his two young daughters sitting either side, trying to rouse her. It broke his heart. When he'd found Sara it had almost killed him too. He didn't want his daughters to have to go through that at such a young age.

'Lily won't wake up, Daddy.'

'Niamh, I need you to hang up the phone.

I'm going to call an ambulance then I'll phone you straight back. I want you to take your sister into another room and wait for me. I'll be home as soon as I can, okay, sweetie?'

'Okay, Daddy.' That little voice, so full of fear, was a sign he had failed his children again. He'd dismissed Lily's concerns about her illness and how it might impact on others, focused on getting what he wanted and nothing else.

She'd tried to warn him of the consequences of getting involved with her, had spent years avoiding relationships through fear of anyone getting hurt. All he'd been able to think about was being with her, giving her the impression they'd deal with anything come what may. He hadn't even asked her how the condition affected her or what he needed to know about it. Now his daughters were suffering the consequences.

Lily was strong. Whatever had happened or caused this blackout, he prayed she would get through it. He phoned for an ambulance on his hands-free device and gave them his address. There wasn't much more information he could give them when he was in the dark himself. All he knew was that Lily needed help and his daughters were there on their own.

His phone rang as he pulled up outside the house. There was no sign of the ambulance so he sprinted towards the front door as he answered it.

'Finn?'

'Lily?' He walked into the living room to see her standing with the phone to her ear.

'Finn, I was hoping to catch you before you left the station. I'm so sorry to have caused all this commotion. Niamh told me an ambulance was on the way so I've cancelled it.'

They both ended the call as they spoke face to face. She looked pale and he wasn't convinced she didn't need some medical assistance after all.

'Sit down. What happened? Where are the girls? They were very upset when Niamh called me.'

'They're in the kitchen having some hot milk and chocolate biscuits. I thought they could use a little treat after the scare I gave them. It was nothing serious. I think it was low blood sugar or something. I hadn't had my dinner before I came around. I'm so sorry.'

'Did you hit your head when you fell? How long were you out for?' Finn knew in the case of a head injury there was a chance of concussion and they couldn't simply dismiss what had happened as a mere inconvenience.

'I have a bit of a lump at my temple but I don't think I was unconscious for very long. The girls were so good phoning you and getting help, even if I don't really need it.' She was trying to convince him he was fussing over nothing but he wasn't taking any chances.

'My number is written down beside the landline in case of emergencies. The girls know they can reach me any time. Let me take a look at that head of yours.' He moved closer to her and she lifted the curtain of hair so he could see the injury for himself.

'Still, I don't know if I would've had the presence of mind to call for help at that age. Ow!' She winced as he brushed his thumb across the raised lump forming under the skin.

'You'll need a cold compress on that. I'm

not sure I've got any frozen peas left. Honestly, you might have to start carrying an ice pack around with you at this rate.' It was the second time she'd had an accident here and he would have to think seriously about leaving her on her own with the girls in case something happened again, for all their sakes.

'I'm sorry we had to drag you away from work for nothing.'

'Better that than coming back to see you being carted off in an ambulance. Are you sure you don't want to go and get yourself checked out at the hospital?'

She shook her head. 'Honestly, I feel fine, and I know all the signs to look out for when it comes to concussion.'

'Well, sit down and I'll bring you a glass of water. I'll just go and see to the girls first.'

'Of course. Tell them I'm fine and I'm sorry I gave them such a fright.'

'I'm just glad it was nothing serious.' Except one day it might be. With the hours he worked, who was to say it wouldn't happen again? Only next time it could be much worse. It might seem heartless but he didn't want to put his girls at risk of the trauma he'd suffered as an adult. Lily understood that. It was exactly why she'd chosen not to have a family of her own and he should have listened to that when she'd told him.

The girls were sitting quietly at the table, clutching their bedtime toys, with their bedtime snacks uneaten. It was obvious to him, if not Lily, that the incident was playing on their minds still.

'Where are my brave girls?' He opened his arms and the two came running at him full pelt for a hug.

Clinging to either side of him, he scooped them up so they rested on his hips, their arms around his neck.

'I'm glad you're home, Daddy.' Niamh buried her head into his chest. Not usually needy, she was clearly needing a little extra TLC tonight.

'Lily fell.' Maeve looked very earnest as she told him about their eventful evening.

'I know, sweetie, but she's feeling much better and she's sorry for worrying you. You did very well, Niamh, phoning me and taking care of your sister, but I think it's bedtime now.' He carried them to their room and deposited them one by one into their beds.

'I was scared, Daddy. Lily was lying on the floor and I couldn't wake her up, no matter how hard I tried.' Niamh was still sitting up recounting the events and it would be a surprise if she got to sleep at all tonight. There were sure to be nightmares and tears and he doubted they'd stay in their own beds for too long, seeking comfort elsewhere.

'I know, honey, and I'm sure it was scary, but you did a good job. Try not to think about it too much. Lily is feeling a lot better. She just forgot to eat tonight and it made her faint.'

'That was silly. She'll get sick.' Niamh's cross face made him chuckle. Clearly his mealtime lectures about eating properly had hit their target. Perhaps he'd have to start monitoring Lily's eating habits too, or distance himself from them altogether.

'I'll tell her. Now, I'll leave the light on so you can read for a little while. I'm going to stay home tonight so you don't have to worry about Lily getting sick again.'

Niamh bounced up off the bed to hug him again.

He was sure he could get cover for one night, not wanting to leave the girls when they were so upset or take a chance that Lily might have another 'turn'.

''Night, you two,' he said, backing out of the room.

''Night, Daddy,'

'Night-night, Daddy.'

Those two little girls were relying on him to keep them safe, to guard them from all the horrors of the world outside those bedroom doors, and he would do everything within his power to do so. He was all they had and they were his world. He couldn't put their peace of mind at risk for anyone. Not even a woman he could be falling in love with. His need for love and companionship and everything he could have with Lily had to take a back seat. He had to prioritise Niamh and Maeve.

'How are you feeling?' He fetched a glass of water before going back into the living room to check on Lily.

She gave him a half smile. 'I've told you, I'm fine.'

'No headaches or nausea?'

'I'm just tired.'

'You can stay in my bed. I'll sleep on the couch.' He felt a responsibility to keep an eye on Lily tonight in case anything else happened. He was unwilling to leave her on her own because it suited him and potentially put her life in danger. Whether what had happened tonight was due to her heart condition or lack of food, she had hit her head and been unconscious. He couldn't send her home in case her condition worsened in any context.

'Don't you have to get back to work? I wouldn't want to get you in trouble.'

'I've got someone to cover for me. I'm needed here tonight. Listen, Lily.' He took a seat across the room so he wouldn't be distracted from what he had to say by the scent of her perfume or the heat of her body. 'Tonight has made me think about what we're getting into. I know you said this was nothing to do with your heart condition but it was enough to scare my girls, for them to worry about you. Niamh should never have had to phone me like that.'

* * *

'I said I'm sorry, Finn.' She didn't need the guilt piled on when she was already beating herself up over it.

'I know it was me who said we can't live our lives based on what-ifs, but I'd forgotten to take my daughters into account and therein lies the problem. When I'm with you I forget about everything else.'

'And you can't take the chance that some day they'll have to grieve all over again. I know.' Tonight was a dizzy spell through lack of food, tomorrow it could be something more serious and he didn't want his children always on alert, worrying that something was going to happen to her. She understood that when it was exactly the way she thought, the way she used to approach life. That caution had been tossed aside the second she'd fallen for Finn.

'Perhaps we should leave things the way they were, on a casual basis.' He was trying to find a compromise, a way of being together without anyone getting hurt, but it was asking the impossible.

'That's not going to work, Finn. I think

this has run its course. You need to focus on your girls instead of being distracted by me.'

'Are you telling me we're over?'

She didn't want to look at his face when she could hear the hurt in his voice. This had been on the cards from the moment they'd got together. At least an early breakup would be easier to get over than another premature death and the girls would never have to know anything about it.

'I think that's for the best. It was only supposed to be a bit of fun and I think we're both past that now.' Somehow Lily managed to get to her feet even though her entire body appeared to have turned to jelly. All of that happiness and contentment she'd experienced in bed with Finn only the night before had now been snatched away from her, leaving her with nothing.

'You don't have to go.' Finn reached out to grab her hand but she didn't want him to touch her in case she made a scene and burst into tears.

She backed away out of reach. 'I do. I've caused enough upset and upheaval for one night.'

'Lily, we can still be friends. You don't have to run away.'

'I don't think we can, and yes, I do.'

She couldn't be around Finn and not think about the time they'd spent together, about what could have been. If it hadn't been for this damn illness blighting her future as well as her present she might have been a part of this family. As always, all she could bring to the relationship was fear and upset. She should never have believed anything else. Then perhaps her heart wouldn't be shattering into a million pieces at the thought of being without Finn and the girls in her life. In the short time she had come to know them, they had become such a big part of her life. They made her happy. Now, even the thought of them made her sad.

She couldn't blame Finn for wanting to protect them. Her foolish mistake had frightened the girls and dragged him away from work, concerned for them all. They couldn't live the rest of their lives like that, worrying, waiting for the day she got really sick. She should know when she'd spent her entire adulthood doing just that. This family had been through enough grief and she couldn't add to it.

On her way out she grabbed her coat and overnight bag from the hall where she'd left them.

'I'm sorry. For everything.'

Finn didn't try to stop her.

CHAPTER TWELVE

'COME ON, NIAMH, your gran is waiting for you,' Finn yelled up the stairs for the third time in an attempt to get his daughter moving.

'I can't find my necklace. I'm not going until I find it.' His eldest's temper as she stormed away from the top of the stairs was probably only a sample of what he had in store for him when she hit her teens.

Finn sighed. 'We may as well get you strapped into your car seat in the meantime.'

Maeve skipped out of the door ahead of him playing with what looked like a lump of kryptonite hanging around her neck. They'd been obsessed with those necklaces Lily had helped them make and he didn't think it was merely because they thought they looked pretty.

He had been fielding questions about Lily ever since that night and why she hadn't been back. It was clear they had built a rapport with her quickly and the attempt to spare their feelings had come too late. Now they were all missing her.

He'd swapped worrying about the future to obsessing over the past. In particular the time they'd spent alone. If he was ever going to think about being with someone again they couldn't possibly hold a candle to Lily. She'd opened up a whole new side of him he'd forgotten existed. If he'd ever really explored it before she'd come into his life.

He'd loved Sara, they'd been together since they were teenagers. She was his first love, the mother of his children and he'd never stop loving her, but he'd had something different with Lily. His relationship with Sara had been expected, their marriage something they'd drifted into because it had seemed the next step to take after being together for so long. Not that he regretted a second of it when it had given him his beloved children.

With Lily he'd found a passion not only for her but for life again too. She'd been understanding about the girls, about the loss of his wife and how afraid he was of them all being hurt again. To the point of leaving him. He hadn't even tried to stop her.

In hindsight, he could have taken the time to research what the condition meant, what he could do to help her and plan ahead. Instead he'd accepted it was over because he was afraid of what it would mean for him otherwise. Now he was lonelier than ever, knowing what he could have had with Lily if he hadn't been so afraid of taking a chance on love again.

'When is Lily coming over again, Daddy?'

'I told you, Maeve, Lily won't be coming over to the house any more.'

'Why?'

'She's very busy,' he lied, clipping his daughter securely into her seat.

Maeve pouted. 'You said we could have a sleepover but we didn't.'

'Lily wasn't well. She wanted to go home to her own bed.' He didn't enjoy lying to his children but what was the alternative—telling them he loved Lily so obviously he'd needed an excuse to push her away? Deep down, he knew that was why he'd acceded to her decision to end things so easily. He'd fallen hard and fast but had been afraid of getting close then being left alone again. The big brave fire-fighter had been frightened by the prospect of love.

'I found it, Daddy.' Thankfully Niamh appeared so he didn't have to keep answering her sister's questions and learning way too much about himself in the process.

'That's good, Princess. Now, get in the car.' He was manning the line for emergency cardiac care tonight and he didn't want to be late. Especially when he'd already had to call for cover recently.

Niamh was admiring her necklace, twisting the piece of sea glass in her hands. 'Isn't it pretty, Daddy. Lily said it was the same colour as your eyes.'

His heart gave an anguished cry at the reminder of Lily in their lives. In a way, despite his efforts, they were already grieving her loss. Not only had she been a great lover and companion to him, she'd been good with the girls. Patient and entertaining and as close to a mother figure, other than their grandmother, as they'd ever hope to find. The possibility of giving the girls a maternal influence, something they would have cherished no matter how long they had together, had been stolen from them.

'It's beautiful, like you.' He dropped a kiss on Niamh's head and hoped that would be the end of the conversation.

'Do you still have your present too, Daddy? Can I see?'

Apparently he'd been mistaken.

'It's here, on my keys.' He dutifully held up his bunch of keys with the homemade fob attached. Now he was cursed forever with the reminder of Lily since the girls insisted on seeing it every time they left the house.

They had presented it to him the next morning after Lily had gone home, upset that she hadn't stayed the night after all. He'd known who'd chosen which piece on sight. The monstrous green rock could only have come from his magpie youngest who liked shiny bling, the sensible dark blue would have been Niamh's choice and the fiery red jewel could only have been from Lily.

He was sure she'd chosen the colour deliberately, a symbol of her feistiness, her passion and the love he'd been too cowardly to admit to, and he hadn't even had the opportunity to thank her.

It was a spurious reason to see her again and he'd be extremely lucky if she would even talk to him, but he was missing her so much that he had to at least try. Anything more than that was probably wishful thinking but maybe, just maybe, she was missing him too and realising what they could have had together if only they'd been as brave in their personal lives as they were in their professional ones.

When the call came in Finn had that familiar rush of adrenaline but also an attack of nerves. Fire-fighting he was used to, it was his job, but he wasn't a heart doctor like Lily. However, they had agreed to attend these emergency medical situations when the ambulance wasn't expected to make it on time. He prayed he would.

'Charlie Finnegan, I'm with the fire service,' he said to the man who'd opened the door.

The frown followed by the look of panic

on the man's face was to be expected in the circumstances.

'It's not the fire brigade we need. I told them on the phone it's my daughter—she collapsed and we can't wake her up.'

'I know. In circumstances like this, where we're able to get to the scene first, we're authorised to provide medical assistance until the paramedics arrive. Now, where's your daughter?' He hustled past the concerned parent with no time to lose if he was going to be able to do anything to help save the child.

'She's in the living room with my wife.'

Finn hoisted his equipment onto his shoulder and headed for the front room, where he found the young girl lying on the floor, covered with a blanket, cradled on her distraught mother's lap.

'Sally? Wake up for Mummy, sweetheart!' the woman cried, but garnered no response.

Finn could see the girl's lips already had a tinge of blue, a sign of cyanosis, meaning a lack of blood flow or oxygen.

He set to work with his equipment. 'I'm Charlie Finnegan from the fire service. As I told your husband, I'm here to offer medical assistance until the paramedics get here.

Now, I'll need you to gently set Sally's head on the floor and give me some space to work on her.'

The mother did as instructed even though she was still very tearful. 'She said she felt dizzy… One minute she was standing there and the next she just collapsed.'

'She has a very fast pulse, that's probably what made her dizzy. This defibrillator will hopefully shock her heart into a normal rhythm.' He opened the child's shirt and attached the sticky pads to her chest.

'Is she going to be okay?' It was the father who asked the question Finn was dreading as he went to comfort his wife.

'We'll do our best to make sure she is.' He was speaking on behalf of himself and the paramedics, though for now it was all on him.

As the device delivered a shock to the little girl's body he thought of his own daughters in the same situation, hovering between life and death. They were all that had been keeping him going since he'd lost Sara, until Lily had come along. With her in his life he hadn't been simply existing but living and enjoying life.

As directed by the voice on the defibrillator, he continued with chest compressions until it was time to deliver another shock.

'Stand clear.'

He thought of Lily lying there some day at the mercy of a machine, with no one else around her. She deserved so much more. Especially when she gave so much of herself to help others, even as far as giving up on the idea of a family to save loved ones from heartache. All she had received in return was rejection and a lifetime of loneliness. Okay, so she mightn't be sitting in every night mourning the loss of their relationship and if there was any chance of getting it back he wanted to try. Life could end at any moment, at any age and it didn't make sense to waste any of it through fear of the unknown.

The defibrillator advised again to begin CPR and Finn focused on the little girl before him. In the midst of the chest compressions he heard the sirens and was relieved that he had done everything he could to keep Sally alive until they got here. He'd had all of the training, of course, but it was a bit like being a trainee again, afraid one wrong move could cause a loss of life.

Finn waited for the defibrillator to reanalyse Sally's heart readings and she suddenly began blinking, a little colour beginning to come back into her features.

'I've got her back,' he yelled to her parents, who'd gone to let the paramedics into the house, and moved Sally into the recovery position.

The group consisting of relieved parents and paramedics came rushing into the room and Finn was able to take a step back.

'Thank you so much.' The father gave him a bear hug which nearly knocked him off his feet.

It seemed trite to say something like 'You're welcome' or 'Just doing my job, folks', so he said nothing other than filling in the first responders with the details of the incident.

He stood waiting with the parents, watching the medical team stabilise Sally, invested in the little girl and the rest of the family. Helping to avoid the pain he and his girls had suffered was a reward for his hard work. Yes, he'd been reluctant at the start of the project, but if this was the outcome, relief instead of devastation, then it could only be a good thing.

Once more his thoughts turned to Lily and how she dealt with people hovering on the brink between life and death every day. She was the bravest, most altruistic person he'd ever met in his life and a man would be lucky to be with her. Or extremely stupid to have pushed her away.

'We're going to transfer Sally to the hospital now. They'll run some tests and work out the best treatment for her.' The paramedics carefully rolled her onto a stretcher and escorted her out to the waiting ambulance. Her parents climbed into the back, holding each other's hands and talking to their daughter, telling her everything was going to be all right.

It didn't seem right to him to simply walk away without seeing this through to the end. As an emergency key worker he knew he shouldn't get personally attached. For peace of mind it was important to be able to separate work life from everything else or he would never be able to switch off his emotions, but this was his first call-out in his new role.

'Do you think I could go with you? I just want to make sure she's all right.' He stopped the driver just as he was climbing into the front of the ambulance.

'Sure. I think you've earned a ride along.'

With the green light to extend his role this once, Finn took a seat up front with the driver. It was only when they were on their way to the hospital, sirens blaring, lights flashing, that he thought about the possibility of seeing Lily again. His own pulse rate began to soar with hope that his relationship with her could be restarted if he worked hard enough on it too.

'Dr Riordan, we have a nine-year-old girl in the emergency department I'd like you to take a look at, if you have time?' The phone call from the consultant in A&E came at the end of Lily's shift. She had nothing to go home for, so one more patient wasn't going to make a difference.

'Sure.' She listened to the summary of the child's presenting symptoms before making her way down to see the little girl for herself. There were a number of conditions which could have caused her tachycardia but they wouldn't know for sure until they ran all of their tests. Whatever the results showed, she would most likely be under Lily's care so she thought it better to get acquainted now, when they were both in the same building.

Since splitting from Finn she'd been spending most of her time at work, trying to keep herself occupied so she wouldn't wallow in her own misery for too long.

Things not working out in her personal life wasn't a new concept but this hurt because she'd got close to Finn's family as well as the man himself. She'd let herself believe it was possible to have it all for however long she was in this world, only for a sharp dose of reality to stab her in the guts.

Being with Finn, her illness had been the last thing on her mind. Somehow he'd made her forget all the bad stuff she thought was her lot in life, to live in the moment. It had been fun until she'd started to believe they could have more than a casual fling. Now she was mourning not only their relationship but the future she'd seen as part of a family. The closest she would ever get to being a mum or having children of her own.

Finn and his girls had already been through a lot with Sara's death, and she represented the possibility of having to go through the trauma of losing someone all over again. She couldn't do that to them. She shouldn't have done it to herself. Lesson learned. Falling for someone wasn't a cure-all, simply a mistake. A painful one it would take a long time to recover from, if ever.

'Hello, I'm Dr Riordan, the cardiologist.' She had to push her own heartache to the background as she walked into the cubicle in A&E.

It was her job to prolong the life of her patients and give them the chance to have everything she couldn't. Scant consolation when she'd had to go back to her old status quo, knowing what she could have had if fate hadn't run up and tapped her on the shoulder to remind her that wasn't her life, it was someone else's. Whether it was the one Sara had left behind or the one a future partner for Finn had waiting for her, it didn't matter.

It shouldn't matter because it wasn't any of her business. Their time had simply been a pleasant interlude and she'd got carried away.

'Hi. I'm John, Sally's dad. Can you tell us what happened or if it's going to happen again?' He was rightly concerned, as was the mum, she supposed, who was sitting by the side of her daughter's bed, clutching her hand.

'That's what I'm here to find out. We're going to admit Sally onto the ward to monitor her overnight and we'll run some tests to see what's going on. Once we have a diagnosis I'll be working with you to give your daughter the right treatment to keep her happy and healthy.' It was a big promise, but one Lily was confident she could deliver. If only her future had been laid out for her the way she hoped to do for Sally, she might not have been so afraid to face it. Now it was too late for her to make up for lost time and lost love.

'We're just grateful that fireman was able to get to our place until the ambulance arrived. If it wasn't for him, Sally might not have made it.' The father was clearly grateful for the intervention, but the new information caused Lily to pause reading the girl's chart.

'A fireman? You must have been a candidate for the new crossover scheme. Glad to see it's working.' She didn't need to brag it had been her baby when knowing it was doing the job of saving lives was sufficient reward. It did, of course, make her curious about who had been the crew member who had saved the little girl's life.

'Yes. He used the defibrillator and did CPR until the ambulance arrived. By all accounts, Mr Finnegan's the one who saved Sally's life.'

Lily's quickening pulse betrayed the idea of her remaining unmoved by the mere mention of the man.

'I'm glad to know the scheme is working the way we intended and that Sally here is doing so well now.'

'We owe him everything,' the mother added and her words brought tears into Lily's eyes from both pride and sadness for the man she seemed destined to be reminded about for ever.

'If you'll just excuse me, I'll go and chase up those blood tests.' She exited the cubicle quickly but the opportunity to get some space from Charlie Finnegan was lost as she ran into him in the corridor.

'Lily? What are you doing here?' He was dressed in the same short-sleeved shirt with the fire department logo and black trousers outfit he'd worn for the photoshoot on the first day the project had launched. It seemed a lifetime ago now.

She cleared her throat before she spoke in case it came out in a squeak. 'I was called down to look in on your young patient, Sally. Her parents have been singing your praises.'

His cheeks turned an endearing shade of pink. 'I just did what I was trained to do. If it wasn't for you I wouldn't have been there at all.'

Whilst Lily appreciated the shared glory, it was killing her standing here making small talk, pretending things were okay, when her heart still felt as though it wasn't done breaking.

'I'm glad it's working. It makes everything worthwhile.'

She went to leave but Finn moved to block her path.

'Can we talk?'

His simple request sent her insides haywire, her stomach in knots and her heart thumping in anticipation of what he had to say. She was too raw to handle it if he said anything nice to her. It would only be another reminder of everything she'd lost, of all the things she couldn't have. She was destined to be the one standing out in the cold for ever, looking in on the cosy family she'd been denied from an early age.

'Not here. We can go to my office.' The busy A&E department wasn't the place for a heart-to-heart over their failed relationship.

Lily ordered up the necessary tests for Sally with a note for the results to be sent to her as soon as they came back.

'Is she going to be okay?' Finn asked as they made their way back up to her room.

'It's too early to say what caused her episode tonight, but I'm sure with the right treatment she'll be able to lead a relatively normal life.' She couldn't believe they were standing in the middle of her office discussing a patient as though they'd never crossed that professional line and ended up in a relationship, no matter how short-lived it had been. Every time she saw him she was going to be reminded of their time together, and how unfair life was that they couldn't still have that. If this was the new normal for them, it sucked.

'That's all any of us want, isn't it?' Finn was looking at her with a strange hangdog expression. He had no right to look at her that way. After all, it was his family she was protecting in all of this.

'Not all of us can have it, though.'

'Why not? Who's to say you can't lead the life you want too?'

'Um…doctors, biology…fate.' It wasn't fair of him to put her through this, upsetting her all over again.

He sighed. 'I know you were just thinking about the girls when you put an end to everything. It's the only real reason I can think of as to why you'd give up on us'

'How are they?' There was no 'us', so she saw no point in referencing it.

'Missing you.'

Another punch in the gut. She was missing them too and didn't need the extra guilt, feeling bad that she'd disappeared out of their lives without a proper explanation. 'That's not fair, Finn.'

'I know, but it's true. We're all missing you.'

'What exactly is it that you want? I'm supposed to be working.' The only way she'd ever been able to protect herself was to keep everyone at a distance and it was about time she returned to her tried and tested methods. Albeit too late to save her poor fragile heart from another blow.

'To say I'm sorry I didn't fight hard enough.'

The vicelike grip his words had on her squeezed the oxygen from her lungs.

'For what?' she managed to gasp with her last breath.

'For us.'

She took a seat at her desk to ensure she didn't give a repeat performance of her dramatic collapse.

'Are you okay?'

'I'm fine. I'm not some delicate flower that's going to fall apart at the slightest touch.' The last thing she wanted was for him to think she was about to collapse again, even if her legs were a little wobbly beneath her.

'I know, you're my Tiger Lily.' He cocked his head to one side and smiled and she was glad she was already sitting down because that would surely have been enough to make her fall to the floor again.

'Not any more,' she reminded them both.

'I know you're still hung up about what happened in front of the girls and yes, it was a shock to everyone but we're over it. There's no reason to keep beating yourself up over it. People get sick all the time. They recover or they live with it. That's life. You don't need to hide yourself away from the world, punishing yourself and those who love you. We can get through this together.'

Love. Together.

The words swam around in Lily's head, making her dizzy and almost steering her off the path she was determined to walk alone.

'I'm moving away, Finn.' She'd toyed with the idea and now, seeing him again, she knew it was the only option. Especially now he was trying to make the impossible work. She couldn't run the risk of running into him at work every now and then, and having this painful reminder of what they'd had every time she saw him.

'What? Where? When?' The heartbroken expression on his face was unmistakable when it was the same one she saw in the mirror every day.

'I think it's best for both of us to make a clean break. I'll look into getting transferred as soon as possible. I'm sure I won't have trouble getting a position at another hospital.'

'So it's not a done deal then? Won't you think about staying for me? I really think we could make it work. I know you care about me, Lily, and you know I love you. At least if we're honest about that, this time we can at least try.'

Finn knelt down beside her chair and took her shaking hand.

'Is this a proposal?' She snort laughed, trying to hide her nerves over what was happening.

'What if it was? What would you say?'

'I'd tell you to stop being stupid. I've told you, I'm moving on and you should too. Who

knows, maybe you'll meet someone else.'
Lily snatched her hand away.

'I don't want anyone else. We're good together, Lily.'

'*Were* good.'

'Tell me you don't love me and I'll walk
away right now.'

'What would that change, Finn? I'm still
me, with all the baggage no one can help me
carry.'

'I should have supported you. I'm sorry I
didn't do more to make you think we could
talk over your fears. I guess I was still trying to protect myself too.'

'Why now? What's happened to cause this
sudden change of heart?' She folded her arms
across her chest, a defensive move against the
words she was afraid would cause more damage to her already battered heart. It would be
easy for her to get carried away by the idea
of living happily ever after again, but reality
had a way of crashing in and spoiling things.
In this moment, in the wake of his life-or-
death encounter with Sally, he might be running on adrenaline and the idea of mortality.
Eventually he would remember hers would

come sooner than most and cause him to think twice.

'Tonight made me realise life isn't guaranteed for any of us. Sally, Sara, the father who died in the fire that night—no one knew what was in store for them any more than we do.' He was gesticulating wildly, his eyes wide, and he was giving off a vibe of absolute excitement, as though he had just made some incredible breakthrough. It was something she'd dared not to search for herself. Hope.

'And if I die and leave you and the girls traumatised? That's what will happen, Finn, we both know it. I've lost my father and my sister, you've lost Sara, and it's something you never get over.'

'That's true, but our time together is something to cherish, isn't it?' He rested his hands on her shoulders, forcing her to look at him. 'Whatever time we have together is precious and we shouldn't waste it when we never know what tomorrow will bring.'

'Have you been overdoing the country songs?' She arched an eyebrow at him, trying to make light of what he was saying, afraid the sincerity she could see blazing in his blue eyes would make her believe it all, but anything had to be better than being alone with this aching hole in her chest where her heart used to be.

'I'm serious. Any of us could go at any time and I don't want to waste another second without you. Sara and I put off a lot of things believing we had for ever. You and I know different, so what's the point in being apart any longer?

'I was afraid of actually admitting that I was in love with you because it meant being vulnerable to getting hurt again. I let you walk away because of my own fears, but I'm willing to take that chance if you are. If you're open to the idea, I'd like to take the next step and for you to move in.'

Lily's eyes almost popped out of her head they were so wide with incredulity at the commitment he was willing to make to her.

'You mean move in with you and the girls?'

'Yes, with me and the girls. I'm not sure you're ready to live with the rest of the crew at the station.'

'I don't know… Some of them are very fit…'

Finn frowned at her before breaking out into a goofy smile. 'I know I'm older, not as fit as the others and have my fair share of issues too, but I love you and I want a future with you. What do you say, Tiger Lily—are you willing to take a chance on love? On me?'

'What if it doesn't work out? What if I get really sick? The last thing I want to do is cause you or the girls any pain.' That went for her too. She didn't want the promise of a relationship, only for him to bail out when things got tough. If that was the case she'd rather be on her own than deal with heartbreak on top of her illness.

'One of the things I've learned about you, Tiger Lily, is that you do everything you can for your patients. You never give up. Now I'm asking you to do the same for yourself, and us, and keep fighting. We can't predict the future and it seems such a waste to throw what we have away on the basis of what might happen. I love you, you love me, and that's all that matters for now. Move in with me and we can build on that.'

Asking her to live with him was something she knew he wouldn't take lightly when it meant being part of his family. Finn would never do anything to hurt his daughters, and that included moving a stranger into their home, into their lives, on a whim. He would have thought carefully about the impact it would have on them by inviting her to stay permanently. It was a huge gamble for him to take and if Lily wasn't prepared to do the same she'd be alone for the rest of her life because she would never love anyone the way she loved Finn.

She thought about the years she'd wasted just existing, the time she'd spent with Finn and the girls, and there was no competition. There was only one place she wanted to be.

'Take me home, hot stuff.'

Finn kissed her long and hard, making up for the time they'd spent apart. When she was in his arms she believed anything was possible and now he was offering her a future together she knew she would fight hard against anything that threatened to take that away.

Her heart might not work as well as some, but it belonged entirely to Finn and if love was enough to keep it beating she'd live for ever.

EPILOGUE

'ARE YOU GOING to be my new mummy?' Little Maeve was standing staring at Lily with her head cocked to one side, face screwed up in concentration.

'Shh. You're not supposed to ask things like that.' Big sister Niamh bustled in with a scolding and tried to wrangle the curious flower girl away.

'It's okay. You're both bound to have questions. This is as big a deal to you two as it is to me and your daddy.' Lily wished Finn were here to be part of the conversation but they had decided not to see each other until the wedding and she didn't want to leave the girls wondering what would happen once they were officially married.

She carefully smoothed her dress before sitting down and patted the bed for the girls to come and join her. They'd spent the night in the hotel room together, with Finn staying down the corridor. Lily's quality time with the girls was always special and they'd had fun putting on face masks and ordering room service.

They always enjoyed girls' nights, something they'd started doing on a regular basis since she'd moved in. It was a way of bonding and they were keeping her young at heart with their endless energy and enthusiasm. Both Niamh and Maeve seemed to be enjoying having another female in the house. Whilst she didn't have much experience with children, she was able to braid their hair and paint their nails, which their father apparently hadn't managed to do adequately since they'd lost their mum.

After only six months of living together Finn had proposed, keen not to waste whatever time they had together. He and the girls had brought her breakfast in bed that morning with a handmade card from the girls with *Will You Marry Us?* written on the front. She'd watched Finn drop to one knee by the side of the bed, holding out a beautiful diamond ring, through happy tears. Of course he'd consulted his daughters before asking when it would affect their lives greatly, and of course Lily had said yes because she loved them all.

Now they were all here in paradise, or Bali to be precise, for their wedding. There was a party planned back home when they returned for friends and colleagues but they'd both wanted the day just for their little family to enjoy. That didn't mean they hadn't gone all out on the outfits. After all, she only planned to do this once.

Not wishing to overdo the frills and froth, she'd opted for a more age-appropriate white satin slip dress, overlaid with a layer of embroidered tulle. Being with Finn had helped her learn to love her body the way it was so she was happy to showcase her best assets in the V-neck of the tailored bodice.

Niamh and Maeve were a big part of the ceremony and the day so they'd had fun choosing their outfits, simple white satin shift dresses with bands around their waists in their favourite jade-green and deep blue colours. They were all wearing the sea glass necklaces they'd made and Lily was looking forward to a stroll along the beach with the girls later to find more treasures.

For now she was content just being here with them, helping them transition into this new family which would include her.

'I'm going to be your stepmother. I'll never replace your mum, but I'll be here whenever you need me. I love you and your dad very much.' She had to choke back the tears, overwhelmed by the occasion and the realisation that she was finally getting that fairy tale ending she'd thought would never happen for her.

'Do we have to call you Mum?' Niamh, the older of the two, who would have had more memories of her mother, asked and Lily wondered how long that question had been bothering her. She'd tried not to force herself into their lives, despite how quickly her relationship with Finn seemed to have moved forward. Thankfully they'd accepted her and she'd done her best to keep the memory of their mother alive so they would never forget the woman who'd brought them into the world.

'You can just keep calling me Lily. Nothing's going to change at home except that I'm going to be Mrs Finnegan now.'

For some reason that made the girls giggle and her heart was full at the sound of them being so happy on such a special day.

'We should go and meet your daddy before he goes and marries someone else.' Lily got up before she started crying and ruined her carefully applied make-up.

Taking the still giggling duo by the hands, she made her way from the hotel down onto the beach.

Finn was standing under the floral arch the hotel had kindly erected for the ceremony. He looked gorgeous in his cream linen suit, sleeves rolled up to show off his tanned muscular forearms and white shirt opened at the neck, giving her a peek at his chest. She couldn't wait to spend the night alone with her husband and thankfully her future mother-in-law was in attendance and taking on babysitting duties tonight.

Lily couldn't wipe the smile off her face as she walked across to meet him at the edge of the sea. It was as perfect a wedding as she could ever have hoped for.

'You look beautiful,' he said as she came to stand beside him and kissed her on the cheek.

'So do you.'

That made him smile but she meant it. Freshly shaven and wearing a suit, or skin smudged with smoke when he was in uniform, he always looked good to her and she knew he always would because she loved him so much.

They said their vows before the celebrant and exchanged rings, then Lily turned to her young bridesmaids.

'I have rings for you too since I'm marrying the whole family today.'

The girls were jumping up and down, fizzing with excitement as she slipped the tiny rings onto their fingers. It was a gesture she'd discussed with Finn to show her commitment to his daughters and a promise she would be there for them. Something she intended to do for a long time.

'I now pronounce you man and wife...and family.'

The celebrant didn't have to give Finn the

go-ahead to kiss her as he took her in his arms and melded his lips with hers. It was difficult not to get carried away when she hadn't seen him since yesterday, but she enjoyed their first kiss as a married couple as much as every other. For the first time in her life Lily considered herself a very lucky woman.

Their smooch was interrupted by a flurry of colourful confetti raining down on them, followed by the joyous sound of the girls' laughter.

'Hey, you two. Come here.' Finn swung the girls up so he had one balanced on each hip and leaned in to give Lily another peck on the lips. Then the girls leaned over to kiss her on both cheeks. Finn's mother, who had shed a tear or two during the ceremony, came over to hug them all.

It had taken a scarred fire-fighter and his family to mend Lily's broken heart so she could finally start living.

* * * * *